Dark-Hearted Desert Men

Many years ago there we............................d as one kingdom—Adama.........................
Adamas apart and the isla......................
The Greek Karedes family...............
Aristo, and the smoldering................
desert lands of Calista.

When the Aristan king died, an illegitimate daughter
was discovered—Stefania, the rightful heir to the throne.
Ruthlessly the Calistan sheikh king Zakari seduced her into
marriage, to claim absolute power, but was overawed by her
purity—and succumbed to love. Now they rule both Aristo
and Calista together in the spirit of hope and prosperity.

But a black mark hangs over the Calistan royal family
still. As young boys, three of King Zakari's brothers were
kidnapped for ransom by pirates. Two returned safely,
but the youngest was swept out to sea and never found—
presumed dead. Then at Stefania's coronation a stranger
appeared in their midst—the ruler of a nearby kingdom,
Qusay. A stranger with scars on his wrists from pirates'
ropes. A stranger who knew nothing of his past—only his
future as a king!

What will happen when Xavian, King of Qusay,
discovers that he's living the wrong life? And who will
claim the Qusay throne if the truth is unveiled?

**Find out more in the brand-new
Harlequin Presents® miniseries**

Dark-Hearted Desert Men

*One kingdom. One crown. Four smoldering desert
princes... Which one will claim the throne—
and who will they claim as their brides?*

Book 1: *Wedlocked: Banished Sheikh, Untouched Queen*
by Carol Marinelli
Book 2: *Tamed: The Barbarian King* by Jennie Lucas
Book 3: *Forbidden: The Sheikh's Virgin* by Trish Morey
Book 4: *Scandal: His Majesty's Love-Child* by Annie West

Dear Reader,

The shifting desert sands, the unforgivable heat of a desert sun and the scent of incense and shisha pipes on the warm, whispering breeze, all combined with a feisty heroine and a golden-skinned hero to end all heroes—what's not to love about sheikh romances?

Which is one reason I jumped at the chance to participate in the DARK-HEARTED DESERT MEN miniseries. How could I say no?

But it was more than that. For to be a part of a series with talented authors Carol Marinelli, Annie West and Jennie Lucas was a chance too good to miss, and there was no way I wanted to miss out on a desert adventure with some of my favorite authors.

Besides, Rafiq and Sera's story had me by the throat from the very beginning. We meet Sheikh Rafiq as a ruthless tycoon, now prince and second in line to the throne of Qusay. On the other hand, Sera is a woman broken by duty and circumstance. Forced together, forced to deal with the still unavoidable attraction in the explosive cauldron of their past, can they ever find the love they once believed they were destined for?

It's fantasy all the way, with a dark-hearted desert man who finally meets his destiny in the shape of a dark-haired woman with an equally dark past. I hope it's a fantasy you enjoy!

Much love, as always

Trish Morey

Trish Morey

FORBIDDEN: THE SHEIKH'S VIRGIN

Dark-Hearted Desert Men

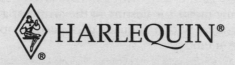

HARLEQUIN®

TORONTO • NEW YORK • LONDON
AMSTERDAM • PARIS • SYDNEY • HAMBURG
STOCKHOLM • ATHENS • TOKYO • MILAN • MADRID
PRAGUE • WARSAW • BUDAPEST • AUCKLAND

Recycling programs
for this product may
not exist in your area.

ISBN-13: 978-0-373-12922-5

FORBIDDEN: THE SHEIKH'S VIRGIN

First North American Publication 2010.

Copyright © 2010 by Harlequin Books S.A.

Special thanks and acknowledgment are given to Trish Morey for her contribution to the DARK-HEARTED DESERT MEN series.

All about the author...
Trish Morey

TRISH MOREY wrote her first book at age eleven for a children's-book-week competition. Entitled *Island Dreamer,* it told the story of an orphaned girl and her life on a small island at the mouth of South Australia's Murray River. *Island Dreamer* also proved to be her first rejection. Her entry was disqualified unread and, shattered and broken, she turned to a life where she could combine her love of fiction with her need for creativity—Trish became a chartered accountant! Life wasn't all dull, though, as she embarked on a skydiving course, completing three jumps before deciding that she'd given her fear of heights a run for its money.

Meanwhile she fell in love and married a handsome guy who cut computer code, and Trish penned her second book—the totally riveting *A Guide to Departmental Budgeting*—while working for the New Zealand Treasury.

Back home in Australia after the birth of their second daughter, Trish spied an article saying that Harlequin Books was actively seeking new authors. It was one of those eureka! moments—Trish was going to be one of those authors!

Eleven years after reading that fateful article (actually June 18, 2003, at 6:32 p.m.!) the magical phone call came and Trish finally realized her dream.

According to Trish, writing and selling a book is a major life achievement that ranks up there with motherhood and jumping out of an airplane. All three take commitment, determination and sheer guts, but the effort is so very, very worthwhile.

Trish now lives with her husband and four young daughters in a special part of South Australia, surrounded by orchards and bushland and visited by the occasional koala and kangaroo.

You can visit Trish on her Web site at www.trishmorey.com or drop her a line at trish@trishmorey.com.

To Romance Writers of Australia, an organization that has taken this one raw writer with a dream, held my hand through the long lean years of rejection, inspired me, educated me and celebrated with me every success along the way.

Most of all, thank you for giving me the best friends a girl could have.

I owe you so much!

PROLOGUE

IT SHOULD have been something to celebrate. Business was booming, the Aussie dollar soaring, and people were buying imports like never before. Combined with a sharp recovery in property prices, Rafiq Al'Ramiz's import business and property investments were doing better than ever.

It *should* have been something to celebrate…

With a growl, he turned his back on the reports and swivelled his leather high backed chair through one hundred and eighty degrees, preferring the floor-to-ceiling views of Sydney Harbour afforded by his prime fortieth-floor office suite to the spreadsheets full of black numbers on his desk.

He didn't feel like celebrating.

What would be the point?

Because it was no fun when it was too easy.

He sighed and knotted his hands behind his head. Challenge had been the thing that had driven him over the last ten-plus years, adversity the force that had shaped him, and for a man who had built himself up from nothing into a business phenomenon, conflict had always been a driving force. Making money when everyone else was, even if he made ten times more than they did, was no achievement. Succeeding when times were tough was his challenge and his success.

Beyond the glass windows of his office the waters of Sydney Harbour sparkled like jewels, passenger ferries jostling with pleasure craft for the perfect view of the Harbour Bridge and the Opera House. For the first time he could remember he felt the insane urge to abandon the office during business hours and take his yacht out and join the pleasure craft taking advantage of the spectacular harbour while the weather was so perfect.

And why not? Business couldn't be better. Why shouldn't he cut himself some slack? He tugged at the knot in his tie, already warming to the notion. He could have Elaine call up that society princess he'd met at last week's charity do. He couldn't remember the cause, or her name for that matter—he was invited to so many of those things and he met so many women—but he could remember the way the blonde had sashayed up to him, so hot in her liquid red dress that she'd all but melted the ice in his glass. His PA would know who she was. That was Elaine's job. And maybe by the time he'd finished with the blonde the economy would have taken a tumble and life might be more interesting again.

He could only hope.

He'd already swivelled his chair back, ready to pick up the receiver and hit the button that would connect him to his PA, when his phone buzzed.

He raised one eyebrow. Elaine had a sixth sense for his requirements, almost uncanny at times, but if she already had the blonde bombshell on line one, her bonus this year would be an all-expenses-paid holiday to the Bahamas.

He picked up the receiver and listened. It wasn't the blonde, and there would be no all-expenses-paid holiday to the Bahamas for his PA, but life was already one hell of a lot more interesting.

CHAPTER ONE

THE sun belted down on the tarmac of Qusay International Airport, the combination turning the air oppressive as Rafiq stepped from the Gulfstream V. He took a moment to let his eyes adjust to the dazzling light, and even over the smell of avgas he breathed it in: the unmistakable scent of his homeland, the salt-tinged air fragrant with a thousand heady spices and dusted with the desert sands that swept so much of the island kingdom.

'Rafiq!'

He smiled as his brother emerged, his robes stark white and cool-looking, from the first of two limousines waiting near the foot of the stairs. At their front, flags bearing the royal insignia fluttered, and four uniformed motorcyclists sat ready nearby, bringing home to him the reality of the bombshell his brother had dropped during his phone call. King Xavian had abdicated after learning that he was really the missing Prince Zafir of Calistan, which meant that his brother, Kareef, would soon be crowned King of Qusay.

Which made him, Rafiq, a prince.

A fleeting hint of bitterness infused his thoughts and senses—*if he'd been a prince back then*—but just as quickly he fought it down. That was history.

Ancient history.

There were far better things to celebrate now, even if the bad taste in his mouth would not disappear completely. He jogged down the stairs, ignoring the heat that seemed to suck the very oxygen from the air, and took his brother by the arm, pulling him close and slapping him on the back. 'It is good to see you, big brother. Or should I call you Sire?'

Kareef waved his jest aside as he ushered his brother into the cool interior of the waiting limousine, the chauffer snicking the door softly closed behind them before sliding into the driver's seat. 'It's good you could come at such short notice,' Kareef acknowledged as the cavalcade pulled away.

'You think I would miss your coronation?'

'You almost missed Xavian's wedding. How long were you here? Three hours? Four at most.'

'It is true,' Rafiq acceded, unable to deny it. Business had been more pressing a few weeks ago—new emporiums opening almost simultaneously in Auckland and Perth, his presence required everywhere at once—but he had managed to get here, only to have his snatched visit cut even shorter with news of a warehouse fire that had threatened some of his employees' lives. 'Although as it turns out he wasn't Xavian our cousin after all. But there was no way I was not coming for your coronation. And if there is one thing I am sure of, Kareef, it's that you are indeed my brother.'

Nobody could have doubted it. The brothers shared the same height and breadth of shoulder, and the same arresting dark good-looks. Those things would have been more than enough to guarantee the family connection, but it was their uncannily blue eyes, eyes that could be as warm as the clearest summer sky or as cold as glacial frost, that cemented the family connection and took it beyond doubt.

'Speaking of brothers,' he continued, 'where is Tahir? Is our wayward brother to grace us with his presence this time?'

A frown marred Kareef's noble brow. 'I spoke with him…' He paused, and seemed to take a moment to gather his thoughts before looking up and smiling broadly. 'I spoke with him yesterday.'

'I don't believe it!'

'It's true. Though it wasn't easy to track him down in Monte Carlo, he's coming to the coronation.'

Rafiq raised a brow as he pushed himself further back into the supple leather upholstery. 'All three of us, back here at the same time?'

'It's been too long,' Kareef agreed.

The journey from the airport through the bustling city of Shafar, with its blend of the traditional low mud-brick buildings amongst modern glass skyscrapers, passed quickly as the brothers caught up on events since they had last seen each other, and soon the limousine was making its way through the massive iron gates that opened to the cobbled driveway leading to the palace. It never failed to impress. In the noon-day sun, the palace glowed like the inside of a pearl shell— so massive, so bright, standing atop its headland, that travellers at sea must be able to see it from miles around, whether in the dazzling light of day or glowing brightly in the pearly light of the moon.

And as the car pulled to a halt under a shadowed portico, and a uniformed doorman swept close and saluted as he opened the door, the reality of recent events hit home once more. Now Rafiq wasn't just entering the royal palace as a member of the extended family. Now he *was* royalty. A prince, no less.

How ironic, when he had built himself up to be king of the business he had created for himself—ruler over his own empire. For now he was one step away from being ruler of the country that had given him birth, the country he had turned his back on so many years ago.

How life could change so quickly.

And once again an unwelcome trace of bitterness sent him poisoned thoughts.

If he'd been brother to the King back then, would she have waited for him? If he'd been a prince, how might things have been different?

He shook his head to clear the unwanted thoughts. The savage heat was definitely getting to him if he was dwelling on things that could not be changed. He hadn't been a prince back then and she had made her choice. End of story.

His brother left him then, putting a hand to Rafiq's shoulder. 'As I mentioned, there are matters I must attend to. Meanwhile Akmal will show you to your suite.'

His suite proved to be a collection of high-ceilinged, richly decorated rooms of immense proportions, the walls hung with gilt-framed mirrors and colourful tapestries of exploits otherwise long forgotten, the furnishings rich and opulent, the floor coverings silken and whisper-soft.

'I trust you will be comfortable here, Your Highness,' Akmal said, bowing as he retreated backwards out the door.

'I'm sure I will,' he said, knowing there was no way he couldn't be, despite the obvious difference between the palace furnishings and the stark and streamlined way his own house in Sydney was decorated. His five-level beachside house was a testament to modern architecture and structural steel, the house clinging to the cliff overlooking Secret Cove, Sydney's most exclusive seaside suburb.

And inside it was no less lean and Spartan, all polished timber floors and stainless steel, glass and granite.

Strange, he mused, how he'd become rich on people wanting to emulate the best the Middle East had to offer, when he'd chosen the complete opposite to decorate his own home.

'And Akmal?' he called, severing that line of thought before he could analyse it too deeply. 'Before you go…'

The older man bowed again, simultaneously subservient and long-suffering in the one movement. 'Yes, Your Highness?'

'Can we drop the formalities? My name is Rafiq.'

The old adviser stiffened on an inhale, as if someone had suddenly shoved a rod up his spine. 'But here in Qusay you are *Your Highness*, Your Highness.'

Rafiq nodded on a sigh. As nephews to the King, he and his brothers had grown up on the periphery of the crown, in line, and yet an entire family away, and while the possibility had always existed that something might happen to the heir they'd known as Xavian before he took the crown, nobody had really believed it. Their childhood had consequently been a world away from the strained atmosphere Xavian had grown up in, even with their own domineering father. They'd had duty drilled into them, but they'd had freedom too a freedom that had allowed Rafiq to walk away from Qusay as a nineteen-year-old when there'd been nothing left for him here.

He'd made his own way in the world since then, by clawing his way up from being a nothing and nobody in a city the other side of the world. He hadn't needed a title then. He didn't need a title now, even if he was, by virtue of Xavian's abdication, a prince. But what was the point of arguing?

After all, he'd leave for Sydney and anonymity right after the coronation. He could put up with a little deference that long. 'Of course, Akmal,' he conceded, letting the older man withdraw, his sense of propriety intact. 'I understand. Oh, and Akmal?'

The vizier turned. 'Yes, *Your Highness*?'

Rafiq allowed himself a smile at the emphasis. 'Please let my mother know I'll visit her this afternoon.'

He bowed again as he withdrew from the room. 'As you wish.'

Rafiq took the next hour to reacquaint himself with the

Olympic-length swimming pool tucked away with the men's gym in one of the palace's many wings, the arched windows open to catch the slightest breeze, while the roof protected bathers from the fiery sun. There weren't any other bathers today; the palace was quiet in the midday heat as many took the opportunity for the traditional siesta.

And of course there were no women. Hidden away in the women's wing, there was a similar pool, where women could disrobe without fear of being seen by men. So different, he thought, from the beach that fronted his seaside property and the scantily clad women who adorned it and every other piece of sand along the coast. He would be a liar if he said they offended him, those women who seemed oblivious to the glances and turned heads as their swimming attire left little to the imagination, but here in Qusay, where the old ways still had meaning, this way too made sense.

The water slipped past his body as he dived in, cool but not cold, refreshing without being a shock to the system, and he pushed himself stroke after stroke, lap after lap, punishing muscles weary from travel until they burned instead with effort. He had no time for jetlag and the inconveniences of adapting to a new body clock, and physical exercise was the one way of ensuring he avoided it. When finally his head touched the pillow tonight, his body, too, would be ready to rest.

Only when he was sure his mother would have risen from her siesta did he allow his strokes to slow, his rhythm to ease. His mind felt more awake now, and the weariness in his body was borne of effort rather than the forced inactivity of international travel. Back in his suite, he showered and pulled open the wardrobe.

His suits and shirts were all there, freshly pressed and hung in his absence, and there were more clothes too. White-as-snow robes lay folded in one pile, The *sirwal*, worn as trousers

TRISH MOREY   15

underneath, in another. He fingered a *bisht*, the headdress favoured by Qusani men, his hand lingering over the double black cord that would secure it.

His mother's handiwork, no doubt, to ensure he had the 'proper' clothes to wear now he was back in Qusay.

Two years it had been since he had last worn the robes of his countrymen, and then it had only been out of respect at his father's funeral. Before that it would have been a decade or more since he'd worn them—a decade since his youthful dreams had been shattered and he'd turned his back on Qusay and left to make his own way in the world.

And his own style. It was Armani now that he favoured next to his skin, Armani that showcased who he was and just how far he'd come since turning his back on the country that had let him down. With a sigh, he dropped the black *igal* back on the shelf and pulled a fresh shirt and clean suit from the wardrobe.

He might be back in Qusay, and he might be a prince, but he wasn't ready to embrace the old ways yet.

The palace was coming to life when he emerged to make the long walk to his mother's apartments. Servants were busy cleaning crystal chandeliers or beating carpets, while gardeners lovingly tended the orange and lemon trees that formed an orchard one side of the cloistered pathway, the tang of citrus infusing the air. All around was an air of anticipation, of excitement, as the palace prepared for the upcoming coronation.

He was on the long covered balcony that led to his mother's suite when he saw a woman leaving her rooms, pulling closed the door behind her and turning towards him, her sandals slapping almost noiselessly over the marble floor. A black shapeless gown covered everything but the stoop of her shoulders; a black scarf over her head hid all but her downcast eyes. One of his mother's ladies-in-waiting, he assumed, going off to fetch coffee or sweets for their meeting.

And then he drew closer, and a tiny spark of familiarity, some shred of recognition at the way she seemed to glide effortlessly along the passageway, sent the skin at the back of his neck to prickly awareness.

But it couldn't be.

She was married and living the high life in Paris or Rome, or another of the world's party capitals. And this woman was too stooped. Too sad.

He'd almost discounted the notion entirely, thinking maybe he hadn't completely swum off his jetlagged brain after all, when the woman sensed his approach, her sorrowful eyes lifting momentarily from their study of the floor.

A moment was all it took. Air was punched from his lungs, adrenaline filled his veins, and anger swirled and spun and congealed in his gut like a lead weight.

Sera!

CHAPTER TWO

HER kohl-rimmed eyes opened wide, and in their familiar dark depths he saw shock and disbelief and a crashing wave of panic.

And then the shutters came down, and she turned her gaze away, concentrating once more on the marble flagstones as her steps, faster now, edged her sideways, as far away from him as she could get, even as they passed. Her robe fluttered in the breeze of her own making, and the scent of incense and jasmine left in her wake was a scent that took him back to a different time and a different world—a scent that tugged at him like a silken thread.

He stopped and turned, resenting himself for doing so but at the same time unable to prevent himself from watching her flight, bristling that she could so easily brush past him, angry that once again she could so easily dismiss him. So many years, and she'd found not one word to say to him. Didn't she owe him at least that? Damn it to hell if she didn't owe him one hell of a lot more!

'Sera!' The name reverberated as hard as the stone of the cloister, no request but a demand, yet still she didn't stop, didn't turn. He didn't know what he'd say if she did. He didn't even know why he'd felt compelled to put voice to a name he'd refused to say even to himself these last ten years or more. He had no doubt she'd heard him, though. Her quickening footsteps were even faster now, her hands gathering her voluminous gown above her feet to prevent her from tripping on its length as she fled.

'Sera!' he called again, louder this time, his voice booming in the stone passageway, although she was already disappearing around a corner, her robes fluttering in her wake.

Damn her!

So maybe he was no more interested in small talk than she was, but there was a time once when his voice would have stopped her in her tracks—a time when she could no more have walked away from him than stopped breathing.

Fool!

He spun around on his heel and strode swiftly and decisively to his mother's apartments. Those days were long gone, just as the girl he'd known as Sera had gone. Had she ever existed, or had she been fantasy all along, a fantasy he'd chosen to believe because it had been the only bright spot in a world otherwise dominated by his father's tyranny? A fantasy that had come unstuck in the most spectacular fashion!

He was still breathing heavily, adrenaline coursing through his veins, when he entered his mother's suite. He was led to one of the inner rooms, the walls hung in silks of gold and ruby around vibrant tapestries, the floor covered with the work of one artisan's lifetime in one rich silk carpet, where his mother sat straight and tall amidst a circle of cushions, a tray laden with a coffee pot and tiny cups and small dishes of dates and figs to one side.

She sat wreathed in robes of turquoise silk, beaming the smile of mothers worldwide when she saw him enter, and for a moment, as she rose effortlessly to her feet, he almost forgot—*almost*—what had made him so angry.

'Rafiq,' she said, as he took her outstretched hand and pressed it to his lips before drawing her into the circle of his arms. 'It's been too long.'

'I was here just a few weeks ago,' he countered, as they both settled onto the cushioned floor, 'for Cousin Xavian's wedding.' He didn't bother to correct himself. Maybe Xavian wasn't his blood cousin, and his real name wasn't Xavian but Zafir, but as children they'd grown up together and he was as much family as any of them.

'But you didn't stay long enough,' his mother protested.

He hadn't stayed long, but it had been the warehouse fire in Sydney that had cut his visit even shorter than he'd intended. He'd made it to the ceremony, but only just, and then had had to fly out again before the festivities were over.

Only now could he appreciate how disappointed his mother must have been. The two years since her husband's funeral had not been hard on her, her skin was still relatively smooth, but there were still the inevitable signs of aging. Her hair was greyer than he remembered, and there were telltale lines at the corners of her blue-grey eyes that he couldn't remember. Sad eyes, he realised for the very first time, almost as if her life hadn't been everything it should have been. Sad eyes that suddenly reminded him of another's...

He thrust the rogue thought away. He was with his mother; he would not think of the likes of *her*. Instead, he took his mother's hands, squeezing them between his own. 'This time I will stay longer.'

His mother nodded, and he was relieved to see the smile she gave chase the shadows in her eyes away. 'I am glad. Now, you will have coffee?' With a grace of movement that was as much a part of his mother as her blue-grey eyes, she poured them coffee from the elegant tall pot, and together they sipped on the sweet cardamom-flavoured beverage and grazed on dates and dried figs, while his mother plied him with questions. How was business? How long was he staying? What items were popular in Australia? What colours? Had he come alone? What style of lamp sold best? Did he have someone special waiting for him at home?

Rafiq applied himself to the questions, carefully sidestepping those he didn't want to answer, knowing that to answer some would lead to still more questions. Three sons, all around thirty years old, and none of them married. Of course their mother would be anxious for any hint of romance. But, while he couldn't speak for his brothers, there was no point in his mother waiting for *him* to find a woman and settle down.

Not now.

Not ever.

Once upon a time, in what now felt like a different life, he'd imagined himself in love. He'd dreamed all kinds of naive dreams and made all kinds of plans. But he'd been younger and more foolish then—too foolish to realise that dreams were like the desert sands, seemingly substantial underfoot and yet always shifting, able to be picked up by the slightest wind and flung stinging into your face.

It wasn't all bad. If there was one thing that had guaranteed the success of his business, it was his ability to learn from his mistakes. It might have been a painful lesson at the time, but he'd learned from it.

There was no way he'd make the same mistake again.

His mother would have to look to his brothers for grandchildren, and, while he had difficulty imagining their reckless younger brother ever settling down, now that Kareef was to be crowned he would have to find a wife to supply the kingdom with the necessary heirs. It was perfect.

'Give it up, Mother,' he said openly, when finally he tired of the endless questions. 'You know my feelings on the subject. Marriage isn't going to happen. Kareef will soon give you the grandchildren you crave.'

His mother smiled graciously, but wasn't about to let him

off the hook. Her questions wore on between endless refills of hot coffee and plates of tiny sweet pastries filled with chopped dates and nuts. He did his best to concentrate on the business questions, questions he could normally answer without thinking, but his heart wasn't in it. Neither was his head. Not when the back of his mind was a smouldering mess of his own questions about a raven-haired woman from his youth, his gut a festering cauldron poisoned with the bitterness of the past.

Because *she* was here, in Shafar.

The woman who'd betrayed him to marry another.

Sera was here.

'Rafiq?' His mother's voice clawed into his thoughts, dragging him back. 'You're not listening. Is something troubling you?'

He shook his head, his jaw clenched, while he tried to damp down the surge of emotions inside him. But there was no quelling them, no respite from the heaving flood of bitterness that threatened to swamp his every cell— and there could not be, not until he knew the answer to the question that had been plaguing him ever since he'd recognised her.

'What is *she* doing here?' His voice sounded as if it had been dragged from him, his lungs squeezed empty in the process.

His mother blinked, her grey-blue eyes impassive as once again she reached for the coffeepot, the eternal antidote to trouble.

He stayed her hand with his, a gentle touch, but enough to tell his mother he was serious. 'I saw her. Sera. In the passageway. What is she doing here?'

His mother sighed and put the pot down, leaning back and folding her long-fingered hands in her lap. 'Sera lives here now, as my companion.'

'*What?*'

The woman who had betrayed him was now his mother's companion? It was too much to take in, too much to digest, and his muscles, his bones and every part of him railed against the words his mother had so casually spoken. He leapt to his feet and wheeled around, but even that was not movement enough too satisfy the savagery inside him. His footsteps devoured the distance to the balcony and, with fingers spearing through his hair and his nails raking his scalp, he paced from one end to the other and back again, like a lion caged at the zoo. And then, as abruptly as he'd had to move, he stopped, standing stock still, dragging air into his lungs in great greedy gasps, not seeing anything of the gardens below him for the blur of loathing that consumed his vision.

And then his mother was by his side, her hand on his arm, her fingers cool against his overheated skin. 'You are not over it, then?'

'Of course I am over it!' he exploded. 'I am over it. I am over her. She means nothing to me—less than nothing!'

'Of course. I understand.'

He looked down into his mother's age-softened face, searching her eyes, her features, for any hint of understanding. Surely his mother, of all people, should understand? 'Do you? Then you must also see the hatred I bear for her. And yet I find her here—not only in the palace, but with my own mother. Why? Why is she here and not swanning around the world with her husband? Or has he finally realised what a devious and power-hungry woman she really is? It took him long enough.'

Silence followed his outburst, a pause that hung heavy on the perfumed air. 'Did you not hear?' His mother said softly. 'Hussein died, a little over eighteen months ago.'

Something tripped in his gut. Hussein was dead?

Rafiq was stilled with shock, absorbing the news with a kind of mute disbelief and a suspension of feeling. Was that why Sera had looked so sad? Was that why she seemed so downcast? Because she was still in mourning for her beloved husband?

Damn the woman! Why should he care that she was sad—especially if it was over *him*? She'd long ago forfeited any and all rights to his sympathy. 'That still doesn't explain why she is here. She made her choice. Surely she belongs with Hussein's family now?'

The Sheikha shook her head on a sigh. 'Hussein's mother turned her away before he was even buried.'

'So her husband's mother was clearly a better judge of character than her son.'

'Rafiq,' his mother said, frowning as her lips pursed, as if searching for the right words. 'Do not be too hard on Sera. She is not the girl you once knew.'

'No, I imagine not. Not after all those glamorous years swanning around the world as wife to Qusay's ambassador.'

The Sheikha shook her head again. 'Life has not been as easy for her as you might think. Her own parents died not long before Hussein. There was nowhere for her to go.'

'So what? Anyone would think you expect me to feel sorry for her? I'm sorry, Mother, but I can feel nothing for Sera but hatred. I will never forgive her for what she did. Never!'

There was a sound behind them, a muffled gasp, and he turned to find her standing there, her eyes studying the floor, in her hands a bolt of silken fabric that glittered in swirls of tiny lights like fireflies on a dark cave roof.

'Sheikha Rihana,' she said, so softly that Rafiq had to strain to catch her words—and yet the familiar lilt in her voice snagged and tugged on his memories. He'd once loved her softly spoken voice, the musical quality it conveyed, gentle and well bred as she was. *As he'd once imagined she was.* Now, hearing that voice brought nothing but bitterness. 'I have brought the fabric you requested.'

'Thank you, Sera. Come,' she urged, deliberately disregarding the fact that Sera had just overheard Rafiq's impassioned declaration of hatred as if it meant nothing. He wanted to growl. What did his mother think she was doing? 'Bring it closer, my child,' his mother continued, 'so that my son might better see.' And then to her son, 'Rafiq, you remember Sera, of course.' Her grey-blue eyes held steady on his, the unsaid warning contained therein coming loud and clear.

'You know I do.' And so did Sera remember him, if the way she was working so hard at avoiding his gaze was any indication. She'd heard him say how much he hated her, so it was little wonder she couldn't face him, and yet still he wanted her to look at him, challenging her to meet his eyes as he followed her every movement.

'Sera,' he said, his voice schooled to flat. 'It has been a long time.'

'Prince Rafiq,' she whispered softly, and she nodded, if you could call it that, a bare dip of her already downcast head as still she refused to lift her gaze, her eyes skittering everywhere—at his mother, at the bolt of fabric she held in her hands, at the unendingly fascinating floor that her eyes escaped to when staring at one of the other options could no longer be justified—everywhere but at him.

And the longer she avoided his gaze, the angrier he became. Damn her, but she *would* look at him! His mother might expect him to be civil, but he wanted Sera to see how much he hated her. He wanted her to see the depth of his loathing. He wanted her to know that she alone had put it there.

Through the waves of resentment rolling off him, Sera edged warily forward, her throat desert-dry, her thumping heart pumping heated blood through her veins.

She knew he hated her. She had known it since the day he had returned unexpectedly from the desert and found her marrying Hussein. She'd seen the hurt in his eyes, the anguish that had squeezed tight her already crumpled heart, the anguish that had turned ice-cold with loathing when he'd begged her to stop the wedding and she'd replied by telling him that she would never have married him because she didn't love him. Had never loved him.

He hadn't quite believed her then, she knew. But he'd believed it later on, when she'd put the matter beyond doubt...

She squeezed her eyes shut at the pain the memories brought back. That day had seen something die inside her, just as her lies and her actions had so completely killed his love for her.

Yet walking in just now and hearing him say it—that he felt nothing for her but hatred, and that he could never forgive her—was like twisting a dagger deep in her heart all over again.

And she had no one to blame but herself.

Her hands trembling, she held out the bolt of fabric, willing him to take it so once again she could withdraw to somewhere safe, somewhere she could not feel the intensity of his hatred. She could feel his eyes on her face, could feel the burn as his gaze seared her skin, could feel the heat as blood flooded her face.

'What do you think?' she heard the Sheikha say. 'Have you ever seen a more beautiful fabric? Do you think it would sell well in Australia?'

At last he relieved Sera of the burden in her arms. At last, with him distracted, she might escape. She took a step back, but she couldn't resist the temptation that had been assailing her since she'd first seen Rafiq again, couldn't resist the compulsion that welled up within herself to look upon his face. Just one glance, she thought. Just one look at the face of the man she had once loved so much.

Surely that was not too much to ask?

Tentatively she raised her lashes—only to have the air punched from her lungs.

Because he wasn't looking at the fabric!

Blue eyes lanced hers, ice-blue, and as frozen as the glaciers that adorned mountaintops in the Alps. So cold and rapier-sharp that just one look sliced deep into her psyche.

And she recognised that this was not the man she had loved. This was not the Rafiq that she had known, the man-boy with the warm smile and the liquid blue eyes, eyes that had danced with life and love—love for her. Oh, his features might other-wise look the same, the strong line of his nose, the cleft jaw and passionate slash of mouth, and the thick dark hair that looked like an invitation in which to entangle one's fingers, but his eyes were ice-blue pits, devoid of everything but hatred.

This man was a stranger.

'What do you think, Rafiq?' she heard his mother say, and a moment later his eyes released their icepick hold, leaving her sagging and breathless and weak in its wake. 'Come, sit here, Sera,' Sheikha Rihana continued, pouring another cup of coffee as she patted the cushions alongside her.

And, while escape would be the preferred option, with Sera's knees threatening to buckle underneath her it was all she could do to collapse onto the cushions and pretend that she was unshaken by the assault his eyes had just perpetrated against her. Maybe now Rafiq would ignore her, for there was no reason for him to so much as look at her again. Hadn't he already made his hatred plain?

Rafiq tried to concentrate on the fabric. He wasn't formally trained in such things, but once upon a time he'd single-handedly selected every item that would be shipped to Australia for sale in his emporiums. Times had changed since those heady early days, and now he had a handful of trusted buyers who circled the Arab world looking for treasures to appeal to his customers, but still he knew something special when he saw it. Even now, while his blood pumped hot and heavy through his veins, he felt that familiar spike of interest, that instant of knowing that what he held in his hands was extraordinary.

'Hand-stitched,' announced his mother, as proudly as if she'd made it herself, 'every one of those tiny gems stitched by hand into place.'

He didn't have to pretend to be interested to indulge his mother; he was genuinely fascinated as he ran the gossamer-thin fabric through his hands, studying the beads, searching for their secret.

'Emeralds,' he realised with surprise. The tiny chips were sculpted and shaped to show off their magnificent colour as if they were the most spectacular gems. The workmanship in cutting the beads would be horrendous in itself, the craft of stitching them to a fabric so light a labour of love.

'Is it not magnificent?' his mother said. 'The beads are fashioned from the off-cuts after the best stones from the emerald mines are cut. This fabric is light, and suited to gowns and robes, but there are heavier fabrics too, suitable for drapes and cushions, of all colours and weights. Could not something this beautiful sell well in your stores?'

'Possibly,' he said, making a mental note to inform his buyers to check it out, and then put the fabric aside, his curiosity once more drawn to the black-clad figure kneeling next to his mother. She was studying the floor again, her long-lashed eyes cast downwards, looking the very essence of meek and submissive. Surely his mother wasn't taken in by such a performance? This was a woman who had married for wealth and privilege and status. She might look innocent and meek, but he knew differently. She was as scheming as she was beautiful.

The thought stopped him in his tracks. Beautiful? But of course she always had been, and even now, with the air of sadness she carried with her, there was a haunting beauty in her slumberous eyes and the curve of her lashes that could not be denied. Beauty and cunning. She had both, like a viper poised ready to strike.

He turned to his mother, only to find her watching him, her eyes narrowed. For a moment he got the impression she was going to say something—could she read his thoughts in his eyes? Was she about to defend the woman again? —but then she shook her head and sniffed, and gestured towards the roll of material instead.

'How can you say possibly? Fabric of this quality, and yet you think it could only *possibly* be good enough to sell?'

'I'll have one of my buyers come over and check it out.'

'Ah, then you may be too late.' She collected the bolt of fabric in her hands, winding the shimmering loose material around it and passing it to Sera. 'I am sorry to have troubled you. Sera, you might as well take this back.'

Sera was rocking forward on her knees, preparing to rise to her feet, when Rafiq reached out and grasped one end of the bolt. 'Stay,' he ordered Sera, before turning to his mother. 'What are you talking about, too late? Why should it be too late?'

Sera looked to the Sheikha, who smiled and put her henna-stained hand over the younger woman's. 'One moment, my child.' And then his mother turned to Rafiq and sighed wistfully. 'There is another party interested and ready to sign for exclusive rights to the collection. If you delay, and wait for your buyer to arrive...' she shrugged for effect '...it will no doubt already be too late.'

'Who is this other party?' But he already suspected the answer, even before his mother confirmed it by giving the name of the biggest importer of Arab goods in the world. Strictly speaking they weren't competitors. He was content to dominate the southern hemisphere while they took the north, each keeping out of the other's way. But to demand exclusivity on a range of goods made right here, in the country of his birth? That had never been part of their unspoken agreement.

He caught his mother's cool-eyed gaze assessing him again,

and allowed himself a smile. It had never occurred to him before, but maybe he owed at least some of his business acumen to his mother. What else could have prompted him to look up a business opportunity while he was here for his brother's coronation but the thrill of the chase?

'I suppose,' he conceded, 'I could go and look at the collection while I am here. Is the workshop here, in Shafar?'

She shook her head. 'No, it is in the town of Marrash, in the mountain country to the north.'

He summoned up a mental map of Qusay, trying and unable to place the town, but knowing that if it was in the rugged red mountains of the north transport would be difficult and by necessity slow. He shook his head. 'Travelling there would take at least a day. It is not practical, given it is so close to the coronation. Is there nowhere in Shafar to view this so-called collection?'

'There is only this one sample here in the palace, but there is plenty of time before the coronation—it is no more than an overnight trip. And you would have to travel to Marrash if you wished to deal with the tribespeople. They would not do business otherwise.'

'But what of Kareef? I have only just arrived in Qusay. What kind of support would I be to my brother if I were to up and leave him a few short days before his coronation?'

'He would think you are a businessman with an eye to business. He would be more surprised if you did *not* pursue an opportunity such as this. Besides, I suspect he will be busy enough with arrangements as it is.'

He supposed she was right. And it was one way of making the most of his time in Qusay. Why not combine business with pleasure? It had been a long time since he had ventured across the desert to the mountains of red stone. A very long time...

'I'll go,' he said, nodding, 'I'll explain to Kareef and get Akmal to organise a driver.'

'You'll need a guide too, to smooth the negotiations.' He was about to protest when she held up one hand softly. 'You might now be a prince, my son, but you are still a man. You will need someone who knows the women and understands their needs, someone who can talk to them as an equal. I would go myself, but of course…' she shrugged '…with so many guests in the palace, and while we wait on news of Tahir, there is no way I can excuse myself. I can send one of my companions. They have all travelled extensively throughout Qusay with me, talking to the women, listening to their needs so that we might better look after our people.'

He noticed the sudden panicked look in Sera's eyes as she sought out his mother's, and wondered absently what her problem was. There was no way his mother would send *her* to accompany him; she knew only too well what his feelings would be at the suggestion. And there was no way he would take her if she did. In fact, instead of looking panicked she should look relieved. With him out in the desert for a couple of days and no chance of running into each other, without the constant resurfacing of memories best left forgotten, she should be relieved. He knew he was.

'Who did you have in mind?'

His mother gestured to a woman sitting patiently in one corner amongst the drapes that lined the walls. 'Amira can accompany you.'

She was older than his mother, with deep lines marking the passage of time in her cheeks, and her spine curved when she stood, but it was the expression of another woman that snared his attention. Sera looked as if she'd just escaped a fate worse than death.

It rankled. He had no wish to spend time with her, but did her relief have to be so palpable? Anyone would think she regarded the prospect of two days in his company with even more revulsion than he did. How could that be possible? It wasn't as if he was the one who had betrayed her. What was she so afraid of—unless she feared that he might somehow try to exact his revenge?

Revenge?

His mother was talking, saying something to Amira, but he wasn't listening. He was too busy thinking. Too busy making his own plans. He looked across at the figure in black, hunched and cowed, her eyes looking everywhere but at him, no doubt wanting nothing more but that he might disappear into the desert with Amira to accompany him.

Did she really find the idea of being with him more appalling than he found the prospect of being with her? The gears of his mind crunched in unfamiliar ways, dredging up memories in their cogs, reassembling them into a different pattern, different possibilities.

Maybe there was something here he could turn to his advantage after all.

She'd never paid for what she'd done. She'd never so much as been called to account. She'd simply turned her back on him and walked away.

Why shouldn't he take advantage of this opportunity to even things up?

'I thank Amira,' he said, turning back to his mother and smiling at the older woman. 'But it is an arduous journey into the mountains that will by necessity be rushed and uncomfortable. I would hate to subject Amira to that. Perhaps I might suggest another idea—someone younger perhaps?'

It was the turn of the older woman to look relieved, while the hunched form alongside his mother tensed, the colour draining from her features. He allowed himself a smile. This might be even more satisfying than he'd imagined.

'Sera can accompany me.'

His mother's eyes turned to him in surprise, but it was nothing compared to the look he saw on Sera's upturned face. Disbelief combined with sheer horror, her black eyes brimming with fear.

An expression he would treasure for ever.

CHAPTER THREE

HE COULD not be serious! 'Please, no,' she pleaded of the Sheikha, who must see the moisture clinging to her lashes, who must know how impossible was the thing he was asking. 'Sheikha, please...'

But, while the Sheikha looked troubled, and squeezed her hand, it was to Rafiq she turned—Rafiq, who looked as if he was about to declare war. 'You are my son,' she said, 'and a Qusani prince. You know I can deny you nothing. But are you sure about this?'

'I have never been more sure in my life.'

'But, Sheikha, please...'

'Sera,' she said with a sigh, patting the younger woman's hands where they lay twisted and knotted in her lap, 'it will be fine. My son is nothing if not a gentleman. You have nothing to be concerned about. Has she, Rafiq?'

And through the screen of her lashes she saw Rafiq smile, the slow, lazy smile of a jungle cat sizing up its next meal. It was a miracle, she thought, that he managed not to lick his lips. She shivered as a chill descended her spine.

'Of course, not. Nothing to worry about at all,' he said, in a steady, measured voice that terrified her all the more for its calm, yet deadly intent.

Nothing to worry about? Then why had she never been more afraid in her life?

* * *

The two four-wheel drives were packed, loaded with water and supplies in case of breakdowns while crossing the vast desert sands on their way to the mountains, and their drivers were waiting. Already a truck had been sent out to make camp where the desert met the sea, where Akmal had recommended they stop for the night before attempting the steep ascent up into the mountains.

Rafiq just shook his head. It almost seemed like overkill, to pack so much for no more than a two-day trip, but he knew from experience that the desert was an unpredictable mistress, fickle and capricious, and as lethal as she was beautiful. Still, he had no plans to prolong this trip, and with any luck the camp would not be necessary. He intended to get there and back as quickly as possible.

Sera hung back, clinging close to where his mother stood in the shade of the porticoed entrance, her eyes, when he did managed to catch sight of them, troubled and pained.

Finally Akmal was satisfied that the last of the provisions had been properly stowed, the engines idling to power the air-conditioning units that would cool the interiors and make the arduous journey through the desert bearable. He bowed his head in Rafiq's direction. 'All is in readiness, Your Highness. Whenever you are ready?'

'Thank you, Akmal.'

'Safe journey, my son,' said his mother, meeting him halfway as he leaned down to kiss her age-softened cheek. 'Take care of Sera.'

'Of course,' he promised. 'I intend to do just that.'

And then he smiled and accepted her blessing, before making for the first car to talk to the driver.

He pulled open the passenger door and saw in the rear-vision mirror his mother holding Sera's hands, their heads close together as his mother uttered a few last words to her. Was she once again guaranteeing her son's good behaviour? Promising Sera that her virtue was safe with him? She needn't bother. Knowing she was uncomfortable in his presence was all the sport he desired. He had no wish to touch her.

He would not give her the satisfaction.

There was a flash of black robes as he saw Sera dash for what she must have assumed was the relative safety of the second car. He allowed himself a smile as he finished what he wanted to say to the driver, before closing the door and raising his hand to his mother one last time before striding towards it himself.

Shock turned her black-as-night eyes wide as he slid into the seat alongside her. A moment later she turned both her face and body away, shrinking against the door as if she might will herself right through it, and his feeling of satisfaction deepened.

She was terrified of him.

Strange how that knowledge had altered his long-held vow. Ten years ago he'd never wanted to see her again. And ever since then he'd always believed that what she'd killed that day was better left buried, his memories of his time with her buried along with it. Being forced to share the same space with her for two days should have been the very last thing on his agenda. And yet seeing her squirm and cower in his presence...oh, yes, this way was infinitely more satisfying than he could have ever imagined.

He took advantage of the space she left, angling himself to stretch out his legs in the space between them, and even though she didn't look, didn't turn, he knew she was aware of every move he made, knew it in the way she shrank herself into an even smaller space.

Oh, yes, infinitely more satisfying.

Why did he have to travel in this car if he needed so much legroom? Sera battled to control her breathing, willing away the tears that pricked at her eyes even as she wedged herself harder against the very edge of the wide seat, squeezed tight against the door, too hot and much too bothered by this man who seemed to think he owned the entire world, if not the entire vehicle. Maybe he did—he was part of Qusay's royal family now—but that didn't change the fact he was going out of his way to make her feel uncomfortable.

But why?

He hated her. He'd said as much to his mother, practically shouted it. He might as well have announced it to the world.

And he knew she'd heard him.

Didn't he think it was enough, just knowing it? Did he think he had to prove it by insisting she come with him, just so he could keep showing her how little he thought of her? Did he have to make her feel any worse than she already did?

Did he hate her that much?

Agony welled up inside her like a mushroom cloud, a familiar pain that tore at her heart and threatened to shred her sanity. But why shouldn't he hate her? Why should Rafiq be any different?

How many times had she been told that she was the one at fault? How many times had she been told that she was worth nothing? That she deserved nothing?

And now Hussein was gone, and still she was hated.

But how could she expect anything else?

And, in Rafiq's case, it was surely no more than she deserved.

'Maybe it's a chance to put the past behind you,' his mother had said when Sera had pleaded one last time to be allowed to stay behind. *'A chance to heal.'* She loved the Sheikha, who had taken her in when she'd had nowhere else to go. She loved her warmth and her wisdom, and the stories she'd shared of her own imperfect marriage. The Sheikha understood, even though what was left of her own family had believed the lies whispered by

her mother-in-law and abandoned her to her fate. Sera trusted her. And yet the past was behind her—long gone. What was the point of dredging it all up? What was the point of reliving the pain? Rafiq hated her. He would always hate her. And who could blame him?

She sucked in a breath, wishing she could concentrate on the passing streetscape as the small convoy left the palace precincts and headed past flat-topped buildings and narrow market streets towards the outskirts of the city, willing her eyes to find something to snag her attention—but it was the reflection in the window that held her captive, the long legs encased in cool-looking linen trousers, the torso wrapped in a snowy white T-shirt that hugged his body where the sides of his jacket fell apart…

She watched him in the window, his long legs sprawled out, his lean body so apparently at ease, and she grew even hotter and tenser as she huddled under her robes.

Curse the man that he hadn't grown old and fat in the intervening years!

She leaned her head against the window and squeezed her eyes closed, trying to concentrate on the warmth of the glass against her cheek and shut out the image of the long, lean body beside her, trying to think of anything but—and still she could see him clearly in her mind's eye. But when would she ever *not* be able to picture him clearly?

Eleven years ago he'd been the best-looking man in Qusay, with his dark-as-night hair and startling blue eyes. Strong-jawed and golden-skinned, he'd won her adolescent heart the moment she'd first set eyes on him. If she could have imagined her perfect man, it would have been Rafiq. Long, muscled legs, broad shoulders, and a chest that had been like a magnet for her innocent hands.

She would glide them around him, and he'd wrap her in his

arms and tell her that she was the most beautiful woman in the world and that he would love her for ever...

Pain sliced through her, deep and savage, old wounds ripping open so jaggedly that she had to bury her face in her hands and cover her mouth to stop herself from crying out. What was the point of bringing it all back? It was so long ago, and times had changed.

Except Rafiq hadn't. He was magnificent. A man in his prime. *A man who hated her.*

'Is something wrong?'

His voice tangled with her thoughts, and she opened her eyes to see that they had left the city behind. Only the occasional home or business lined the bitumen highway out of the city, the landscape giving way to desert as they headed inland.

Two days she must spend in his company, and he had to ask if something was wrong? What did he think? 'I'm fine,' she answered softly. There was no point saying what she really thought or what she really felt. She'd learned that lesson the hard way.

'You don't look fine.'

She bit her lip, refusing to face him, gathering her robes a little tighter around herself, resenting the fact he wouldn't just let her be. It was true she would feel better if he wasn't right there next to her, brooding and magnificent at the same time. And she would feel much better if the air didn't carry the faint hint of his cologne, seductive and evocative. But right now she was stuck with both, and there wasn't one thing she could do about it but survive. And if there was one thing Hussein had taught her to be good at, it was survival.

'I am sorry to offend.' She folded her hands in her lap and sat up straighter against the leather upholstery, watching the desert speed by.

What had happened to her? This was not the Sera he knew.

Or had she always been destined to turn into this bland, cowering shadow of a woman? Had her character been flawed from the very beginning and he'd been lucky to escape from her clutches when he had? Would he now be regretting it if she hadn't found a higher-ranking, more wealthy target to get her claws into? Wouldn't that be ironic? He was a prince now. What would that have meant to a woman who had married for wealth and prestige? Maybe there was another reason for her to look so sullen—mourning the big fish she had inadvertently thrown back and that had got away.

He sat back in his seat, the Arabic music the driver had found on the radio weaving patterns through his mind, giving birth to yet another unsatisfactory line of thought.

For, whatever troubled her, and however her mind worked, she was closing him out again, fleeing from him in mind and spirit as surely as she had fled from him in the stone passageway. Was this her tactic, then, to stay silent in the hopes he would leave her alone?

Not a chance.

He hadn't dragged her out here simply so she could cower in a corner and pretend he wasn't here.

'How long have you been with my mother?'

He caught her sigh, felt her resignation and more than a hint of resentment that she would not be able to avoid answering his questions, and was simultaneously delighted that his tactic was working and annoyed at her reaction. Was it such a chore for her to be with him? Such an imposition? Once upon a time she would have turned and smiled with delight at the sound of his voice. She would have slid her slender hands up his chest and hooked them around his neck and laughed as he spun her slim body around, laughed until he silenced her laughter with his kisses.

Once upon a time?

Since when did nightmares start with 'once upon a time'?

'How long?' he demanded, when she took too long to answer.

Tentatively she turned her head towards him, her gaze still hovering somewhere around his knees. 'A year. Maybe a little longer.'

'I didn't see you at Xavian's—*Zafir's*—wedding. But you must have been in the palace then.'

'I chose not to go.'

'Because I was there?'

Her eyes flicked up to his. Skittered away again just as quickly. 'Partly. But my h… Hussein's family were also in attendance. And some of his associates. It was wiser for me to keep my distance.'

He wondered why she had hesitated over calling him her husband. But if he was honest he was more annoyed that it wasn't his presence that had kept her away. 'You don't get on with them?'

She seemed to consider his question for a while, sadness welling in her eyes. 'It is easier for all concerned if I remain in the background.'

He took it as confirmation. 'And so my mother took you in.'

She nodded, the long dark curve of her lashes fluttering down. She was all about long lines, he realised. Always had been. Still was. The long sweep of her lashes, the smooth line of her high cheekbones and the sweeping curve to her jaw, the generous symmetry of her lips.

And maybe for now the rest of her was hidden under her voluminous robe, but he remembered how she looked. How she felt under his hands and the way she moved. Though the robe covered her completely, he knew she was little changed from those days.

His head rocked back, his hands raking through his hair as he was overcome by the sheer power of the memories of the past.

She could have been his. She *should* have been. She had

already been part of him, as much a part of him as breathing, and he could have had her—all of her. Oh, God, and he'd been tempted…so tempted. And in the end only the vow he'd made had held him back.

Because she'd been so perfect. And he'd wanted everything to be right for her. He'd wanted everything to be as perfect as she was. And for that reason he had not touched her that way. Not until their wedding night, when they could be united for ever. Legally and morally.

Body and soul.

A wedding night he had wanted and planned and longed for with all his heart. A wedding night they had never had.

Because she'd given herself to someone else first.

God, what kind of madness had made him think he was ready to face again the woman who'd done that to him?

He brought his head back down on an exhale, opened his eyes and saw her watching him, her dark eyes so filled with concern that his fingers stalled in his hair. *Damn it, he didn't want her sympathy!* He let his hands drop into his lap.

Her eyes followed the movement, a frown marring her perfect brow. 'Are you all right?'

And it took him a breath or two until he was sure he was back in control, until he'd clamped down on the memories of heated kisses and shared laughter, of silken skin and promises of for ever that had come surging back in such a tidal force of emotion, the feelings that had lain buried for so long under a concrete-thick layer of hatred.

'Jetlag,' he lied, his voice coarse and thick, and designed to close off all conversation as he turned away to stare unseeingly out of his window.

CHAPTER FOUR

TWO hours out of Shafar the cars turned off the highway, heading along a sandy track through the desert. They would meet up with the narrow coast road much further on, where the track met the coastline, and where their camp should be ready for them if they needed to stop.

The going was tougher here, and the cars ground their way over the uneven and sometimes deeply rutted track, their passengers bouncing upon the upholstery as the car jolted them around. Far ahead they could just make out the smudge on the horizon that marked the beginning of the red mountains, where they were headed—a smudge that slowly grew until their jagged peaks rose high in the windscreen as they made progress over the bumpy and desolate terrain.

They stopped further on for a break at a welcome oasis, the cars pulling under the shade of a stand of date palms, the passengers more than ready to rest their jolted bones. A short break now and they would still make Marrash tonight, leaving enough time tomorrow for the necessary inspections and at least the preliminary negotiations. If all went well they would be back in Shafar no later than tomorrow evening.

Sera climbed from the car, happy to stretch her legs, but even happier to escape the hothouse atmosphere in the back seat for a few minutes. Her temples and neck promised the onset of a tension headache. Even the fiery ball of the sun and the super-heated air was some kind of relief. She knew it would only be a matter of time before he'd find another angle of attack, another means to criticise her and find fault, but for now she'd had enough of the brooding silence and the constant anticipation of yet another volley.

The drivers were busy pulling things from the backs of the vehicles, organising refreshments and checking the vehicles, their conversation like music on the air. Rafiq was there too, she noticed, wanting to help even over their protests that they should be serving him.

She walked towards the inviting pool, breathing a sigh of relief, certain he wouldn't listen—not if it meant the alternative was spending more time with her. Which meant that at least for a few blessed minutes she had some space to herself.

The oasis was small, no more than a scattering of assorted palms clustered around a bubbling spring that spilled into a wide pool, with an ancient stone shelter to protect travellers caught in the sandstorms that rolled from time to time over the desert that surrounded them on all sides. A tiny slice of life in the midst of nothingness. And there *was* life. Tiny birds darted from bush to bush, and brightly coloured butterflies looked like flowers against the dark green foliage. Immediately Sera felt more relaxed, felt the peace of the oasis infuse her veins.

Rafiq had sat like a thundercloud beside her, silent and threatening, ever since that moment in the car. Sera had recognised the change—as if something unseen had shifted in the space between them, as if he too was remembering a time that both of them would rather forget. Whatever it was, Rafiq hadn't welcomed it. She'd witnessed the turmoil that had turned his cool eyes to the troubled blue of a stormy sky; she'd felt the torment she'd seen there as if it were her own. She'd recognised it.

The water in the pool beckoned, crystal-clear and inviting. She knelt down in the long reedy grass at the water's edge, trailing her fingers through the refreshingly clear water, pouring some over her wrists to cool herself down, patting some to her throbbing temples. She sighed with relief.

It was too much to expect that it would last—they couldn't stop long—but right now, it was bliss.

A plume of sand rising from the desert drew Rafiq's attention. He shaded his eyes from the sun and peered into the distance, where the mountains now loomed in jagged red peaks. The billowing sand drew closer. It was too early to hear the car, but no doubt they would soon have company.

He swung his eyes around, to the place he'd been studiously avoiding up till now, to the place where Sera sat serenely at the water's edge, eyes closed, her face turned up towards the sky in profile, her features for once at peace. Without thinking his feet took him a step closer. She'd loosened the scarf around her head and her glossy black hair flowed down her back, shining blue in the same dappled light that moved shadows across her satin skin and showed off the silken curve of her throat.

And something shifted deep inside him. She was still so beautiful. Dark lashes kissed her cheeks, and the curtain of black hair hung in a silken stream over her shoulders and beyond, and her generous mouth held the promise of a kiss. In the dry heat, his blood started fizzing. Eleven years after she'd married someone else, he still thought her the most beautiful woman he'd ever seen.

And under the robe? Would she still be as perfect as he remembered? Would she still feel as satin-skinned in his hands? Would she still melt into his touch as if she was part of him?

He took another step closer before he heard the car, before the sound filtered into his brain and he realised what he was doing. He looked back at the source of his confusion. What the hell was wrong with him? The sun must be getting to him.

But Sera had heard the sound too, her head swinging around, but her dark eyes' mission forgotten when they found him watching her. She swallowed. He followed the upward movement of her chin, followed the movement in her throat, knew the instant she'd taken her next breath.

Even across the space between them he was aware of every tiny movement, every minute change in her eyes, in the flare of her nostrils. And as he watched her, and as she watched him, the dry air crackled between them like fireworks.

Until above it all he heard voices and the sounds of an engine, brakes squealing in protest, and he spun away, his mind and his senses in disarray.

It was a relief to see that some things still made sense. A four-wheel drive had pulled up at the oasis in a cloud of sand. A distraction. Thank God.

The driver emerged, cursing and gesticulating wildly, while a woman climbed wearily out of the other side, reaching into the passenger seat behind and removing first two dark-haired toddlers and then a tiny baby from their seats in the back. She herded the small children before her towards the pond, her voice a slice of calm over motherly panic as she clutched the baby, even as the man opened the hood and let loose with a new string of invective.

Steam poured up from the engine. The man flapped his hands uselessly, then clutched at the side of his white robe with one hand and simultaneously reached for the radiator cap.

It was Rafiq who stopped him, Sera saw. Rafiq who was there first, stopping his hand, urging him to wait. Their drivers followed, reiterating his advice, and she looked back as the woman neared, her toddlers stumbling before her, the crying baby clutched tight in her arms.

'Be careful!' the mother called out, following as fast as she could. 'Stop before you reach the water.'

Sera was only too happy to assist, stretching out her arms to form a barrier that the twin girls collapsed into at the last moment, laughing and shrieking, thinking it was a game. The mother breathed a sigh and thanked her, before settling with her brood at the water's edge, taking the time to make the traditional greetings even as she settled her baby to feed now that she knew her other children were safe.

Sera smiled, her spirits lifting at meeting Aamina and her children. A visitor was a welcome distraction—especially a young mother with such a young and energetic family. The woman had a beautiful round face, and a generous smile that persisted patiently, even when the children got too excited and jostled the feeding infant impatiently in her arms. Only the shadows under her eyes betrayed how much she yearned for sleep. Sera was plagued with shadows under her eyes too, she knew, but she could only wish they were for the same reason. But this woman was so young, and yet already with three children…

That could have been her, she thought, in a sudden and selfish moment of madness that had no place or no relevance in her real world, and yet which still refused to give way to sanity.

That could have been her if she'd followed her heart and not her head.

If she'd ignored her family's demands and the threats made against them.

That could have been her if she'd married Rafiq.

Sera clamped down on the unwelcome thoughts. Because that was all in the past, and marrying Rafiq had never been an option, not really, no matter how much she had wanted it, and she couldn't blame her family alone.

It was pointless even thinking about it, no matter how much Rafiq's return to Qusay had made her wonder how things might have been if she'd made a different decision all those years ago.

Instead she tried to focus on the young woman's story, and

why she was here now, travelling across the desert with such a tiny infant. It was not ideal, the woman acknowledged, but necessary, as her husband's mother was seriously ill in hospital in Shafar, and they had promised to take their new baby, named Maisha in her honour, to meet her. But her husband was impatient, and had been pushing their aging vehicle too hard. It was lucky they had made it as far as the oasis before the radiator had blown completely.

The toddlers, no more than eighteen months old, had been content to wait at their mother's side while she fed the baby, but now demanded more of their mother's attention. They wanted to paddle in the shallows, and they wanted their mother to take them. Both of them.

Their mother looked lost, though the babe at her breast had thankfully finished feeding and was now sleeping, and Sera could see the woman was trying to work out how to juggle them all.

'Mama, plee-ease,' the toddlers insisted, and their mother looked more conflicted than ever.

'I could hold the baby,' Sera suggested, 'if it might help?'

And the mother looked at her briefly, taking less than a second to decide whether to entrust this stranger with her tiny baby before making up her mind. She smiled, propping the baby up on her shoulder and patting its back. 'Bless you,' she said.

The baby joined in with a loud burp that set the girls off with a fresh round of giggles. The girls' laughter was infectious, and Sera found herself joining in the glee before the mother passed the baby over to her waiting arms. The infant squirmed as it settled into the crook of her arm, nestled into her lap, while the mother swooped her robe over one arm and kicked off her sandals, her own smile broadening. She held a twin's hand securely in each of her own, and the trio ventured gingerly into the water, the girls shrieking with delight as they splashed in the shallows.

In her arms the baby stirred and sighed a sigh, blowing milky bubbles before settling down into sleep, one little arm raised, the hand curled into a tiny fist. So tiny. So perfect. Sera touched the pad of one finger to its downy cheek. So soft.

She smiled in spite of the sadness that shrouded her own heart—sadness for the missed opportunities, the children she'd never borne and maybe now never would, and ran her fingers over the baby's already thick black hair, drinking in the child's perfect features, the sooty lashes resting on her cheeks, the tiny nose, the delicate cupid's bow mouth squeezed amidst the plump cheeks.

So utterly defenceless. So innocent. And then her mind made sense of it all. Maybe it was better that she'd never had children. After all, she'd proved incapable of even taking care of her own tiny kittens.

The children laughed and splashed and squealed in the shallows, and the baby slept on, safe in Sera's arms.

When one of the drivers laid out a blanket with refreshments for them, and the children whooped and fell on the picnic, their hunger now paramount, Sera told the mother to look after the girls first. Once again the mother smiled her thanks as she helped her hungry toddlers feast.

Not long after, with the radiator cooled and refilled, their car was pronounced fit to go and the mother thanked Sera as she scooped her sleeping infant back into her arms. 'But you haven't had anything to eat yourself yet,' she protested, as the remains of their quick repast were already being cleared away.

'It doesn't matter,' Sera replied honestly, for the woman had given her a greater gift—the feel of a newborn in her arms and the sweet scent of baby breath.

Although that gift had come with a cost, she realised, as she waved the mother and her children goodbye, smiling as she wished them well in spite of the tears in her eyes. She'd almost forgotten in the past few years how much she'd wanted children. She'd almost come to terms with the fact she might never have them.

And right now that reawakened pain was almost more than she could bear.

She turned and walked slowly towards the pool again, the sadness squeezing her heart until she was sure it would bleed tears.

She sniffed down on her disappointment, willing it back into the box where she'd kept it locked away until now. They would be resuming their journey shortly; the drivers were already making their final checks of the vehicles and re-stowing their gear. Rafiq had thankfully kept his distance while the woman and her children were here, but soon she would have to put up with his thundercloud-dark presence again. She needed to get herself under control before then.

Rafiq looked at the map one more time, trying to focus, trying to assimilate what the father of the small family, a local, had informed them—that the mountain track up to Marrash had suffered in recent landslips and that progress could be slower than they expected.

It was news Rafiq hadn't wanted to hear, for it meant that there was a chance they mightn't make Marrash tonight. The local man had advised that it would be madness to try to negotiate the treacherous mountain road in the dark. Both drivers had agreed, suggesting that perhaps they should make use of the camp at the coast. The truck that had set out earlier would have prepared for their arrival, and the camp was even now being readied for them.

But he didn't want this trip taking any longer than one night, and if they stopped tonight and negotiations in Marrash took too much time they might well have to spend a second night at the camp, so he'd argued that if they cut their break short and pressed on now they could still be in Marrash by nightfall.

He didn't want to run the risk of having to spend two nights away from the palace.

And it wasn't only because he had to get back for the state banquet being held in Kareef's honour.

He gave up pretending to study the map and looked over to the pool, where the real source of his irritation sat at the edge, gazing fixedly at…

He tried to follow her line of sight, but there was nothing but sand beyond the fringe of trees and nothing to see.

He'd thought this trip would be so easy, that he would be the one irritating her, but her presence was akin to the rub of sandpaper against flesh, the continual abrasion stinging and ferocious on flesh raw and weeping, and he wondered about the sanity of making this journey at all. Would not his business survive without his hunting down a fabric made by some village high up in the mountains? And it could still be a wild goose chase. He didn't even know at this stage if he was all that interested.

It was bad enough that he would be forced to spend the next twenty-four hours with her. The last thing he needed was to spend more because of the parlous state of the roads. He would speak to Kareef about those. For all Qusay's wealth from its emerald mines, and the wide highways leading out of the city, there remained plenty of places where money could be used. The roads in this part of the desert were definitely one of them.

He growled his irritation and looked back at the map. Just as quickly he looked back again, frowning this time. For she looked sad again, her expression hauntingly beautiful, but sad all the same.

He'd seen her smile when she'd been holding the child, and he'd even heard her laughing—or had he just imagined that? But she'd definitely smiled. He had seen her face light up, filled with love as she had rocked the sleeping baby in her arms.

It had been hard to look away then, because for a moment,

just a moment, he had seen the face of the girl he had fallen in love with.

'*She is not the girl you once knew.*'

Like a blow to the body, his mother's words came back to him in a rush.

No, she was not the girl he'd known before. She was a widow now.

Hussein's widow.

Impatiently he tossed the map aside. Regardless of the advice from their visitor, they would have to get going. He was determined to make Marrash this evening.

She started as he drew close, her eyes widening in surprise as he approached, before her head dipped, her gaze once again going to the ground. 'Is it time?'

Her voice was serenity itself, and he knew the shutters were back, slammed ever so meekly and serenely, but nevertheless slammed effectively in his face. What would it take to shake her up? What would it take to shake her out of that comfort zone she retreated to every time he so much as looked at her?

'I always thought you wanted a big family—six children at least.'

There was a rapid intake of breath, a pause, and he wondered if she was remembering that very same day, when they'd raced their horses along the beach, hot rushing air accompanied by the splash of foam and the flick of sand, their mounts neck and neck along the long sweep of coast. And finally, with both horses and riders panting, they'd collapsed from their mounts' backs onto the warm sand and shared their dreams for their future together. '*A big family,*' she'd said, laughing, her black hair rippling against the arm her head had nestled against. '*Two boys and two girls, and then maybe one or two more, because four will surely not be enough to love.*'

And he'd pretended to be horrified. '*So many children to*

provide for! So many children to love. Who will have time to love me?'

And she'd leaned over him and brushed a lock of hair from his brow, her hand resting on his cheek. *'I will always love you.'*

He still remembered the kiss that had followed, the feel of his heart swelling in his chest with so much joy that there had been no room left in his lungs for air. But he hadn't needed air then—not with her love to sustain him.

More fool him.

'Maybe,' the woman before him finally admitted, dragging him back to the present. 'Maybe once.'

'And yet you never had children of your own.'

Her hands wrung together, her bowed head moving from side to side, agitated, as if his line of questioning was too uncomfortable, as if looking for a means of escape. He wasn't about to provide it, not when he needed so many answers himself.

'Why not?'

Now the movement of her head turned into a shake. One hand lifted to her forehead to quell it, and her voice, when it came, was nowhere near as steady as she would no doubt wish. 'It… It didn't happen.'

'Didn't Hussein want children?'

Her agitation increased; her eyes were raised now, and appealing for him to desist. 'Why does it matter to you? Why can't you accept it? It just didn't happen!'

'What a waste,' he said, not prepared to give up yet—not when there were so many unanswered questions and when she looked so uncomfortable. 'Because I saw you with that baby.' She looked up at him, her eyes wide, suddenly vulnerable, as if wondering at this change of tone. 'You looked good with it. I always thought you would make the perfect mother.'

Her mouth opened on a cry, and she snapped it shut, turning

her head away, but not quickly enough that he could miss the moisture springing onto her lashes.

'Did you love him?' Anger surged in his veins like a flood tide. Was that why she was crying? Because she'd wanted her husband's children so desperately and she would forever mourn not having them? It pained him to ask, but he was here with her now, and somehow it was more important than ever that he know the truth. 'Did you love Hussein?'

She squeezed her eyes together, and then near exploded with her answer. 'He was my *husband*!'

Her words sparked a short-circuit in his brain. 'Tell me something I don't know!' he said, snapping back with equal ferocity, his voice as raw as his emotions. 'I was there—remember? One year in the desert I had to endure, to learn the skills to be a man, but one month in and all I learned was that I couldn't survive without you, that I needed to be with you. But you couldn't wait one year. In fact, you couldn't even wait four short weeks!'

She dropped her face into her hands. 'Rafiq, please—'

'And I found my would-be bride, all dressed up in her wedding finery, the most beautiful bride I could ever imagine, and for a moment—just one short, pathetic moment—I thought that you had somehow known I was returning. And that this was to be the day we would be bound together as man and wife for ever.' He looked down at her, his fury rising, seeing only the vision of her back at the palace, a gown of spun gold clinging to her slim form, row after row of gold chains around her neck, her dark kohl-rimmed eyes wide with shock as he appeared in the doorway, the cry rent from his lungs, the cry of a beast in agony. 'But it was not to be our day, was it? Not when you were standing at the altar ready to marry another man!'

'Rafiq,' she said softly, and he recognised her trying to

reason with him when he knew there was no reason. 'It wasn't supposed to happen that way. But… But I had no choice.'

'You had a choice! You chose Hussein. You chose life as a wealthy ambassador's wife over life with me.'

'Please, that's not true. You knew my father had promised me to him. You knew it could happen.'

'While I was away? Yes, there was talk of an arrangement. But you saw me leave for the desert for a year. You let me go. You kissed me goodbye, promised that you would be waiting for me on my return and that we would overcome our families' objections. I thought you would be strong enough to wait that long. But you were too much of a coward. I had no sooner disappeared from sight before you formalised the arrangements to marry Hussein behind my back.'

'It wasn't like that!'

'No? Then what *was* it like?'

She raised her face to the sky and shook her head from side to side. 'What did you expect me to do? I had seen what happened after my best friend Jasmine returned from the desert, close to death, because she and your brother had chosen to defy their parents' wishes for their future.'

She paused, remembering Rafiq's father and how he had laughed at her when she had protested at marrying Hussein, pleading that she had promised to marry Rafiq. *'I will choose my sons' brides,'* he had decreed. *'Look at the mess Kareef has made of his life. That will not be allowed to happen to Rafiq.'* She swallowed back on the memories. How could Rafiq pretend not to understand?

'How could I do the same to my family—*to yours!*—after that? How could I shame them that way when I had seen what it had cost everyone?'

He brushed her words aside. 'You told me you loved me!'

'I know, but—'

'Which is why you married Hussein when I had been gone less than a month. *Because you loved me!* What a total fool you made of me.'

'Rafiq, please, you must listen…'

'Do you know how I felt standing there? Do you have any idea what it was like to have everyone's eyes upon me, to have your father and Hussein openly sneering in victory, others filled with pity, feeling sorry for me, poor Rafiq, the last one to know what everyone else had known all along. That you never had any intention of marrying me.'

She shook her head. 'I didn't mean—'

'But even that wasn't enough for you, was it? Because, not content with simply humiliating me in front of the entire palace, you then had to grind my love into the dirt!'

She shook her head again, one hand at her brow, the other over her mouth, and he wanted to growl and shake her. If there was a prize for affectation, a prize for acting melodramatic, *pretending that she cared*, she would win it hands-down. 'I didn't want to hurt you.'

He snorted his disbelief. 'Like hell! You delighted in it. Because when I pleaded with you, when I begged you to halt the wedding, to tell me —to tell everyone—that it was me you loved and not Hussein, you looked me in the eye and told me and everyone else there that you had *never* loved me.' His chest heaved, his breath ragged and rasping, as if the muscle that was his heart was remembering that day and the pain that had torn through it, leaving it in tattered shreds. 'Tell me, then, that you didn't love Hussein.'

Silence met his demands, with only the sound of their laboured breathing filling the space between them, the low rumble of the idling engines coming from the vehicles nearby. Under the shade of the palms the drivers squatted, waiting, sipping coffee and keeping their distance, knowing their business was not to interfere, even though they could certainly hear their raised voices, and even though Rafiq himself had pressed upon them the urgency of moving on.

'Oh, Rafiq,' she whispered, reaching out a tentative hand to him, a hand that wavered in the air before it dared land on his skin.

He scowled at it as he might regard some annoying insect, ready to slap it away.

'Rafiq. I…I'm so sorry.'

She was sorry? She had done all that she had done and all she could find to say to him was that she was sorry? She had humiliated him, stomped all over his teenaged hopes and dreams, thrown his life into total disarray, and she was *sorry*?

Blood pounded in his veins, crashed loud in his ears, and when he closed his eyes it was blood-red that he saw behind his lids. 'You're sorry? What exactly are you sorry for? That you lost your rich husband, your entrée to the party capitals of the world? Or that you married him and missed out on landing an even bigger fish? You could have been sister-in-law to the King if you'd waited like you'd promised and married me. How would that have been? All that prestige. All that pomp and ceremony to lap up.

'Except back then you didn't know my brother was going to be King, did you? So you chose someone older, someone rich. You chose Hussein and a guaranteed good life. The high life. Well, I hope you're enjoying life, Sera, because I sure am. The last thing I needed was someone like you, no better than a gold-digger in search of a dynastic marriage. If Hussein were still alive I'd shake his hand right now. He saved me from a fate worse than death. Marriage to you.'

'No! Rafiq, don't say that!' Her face was crumpled now, liquid flowing freely from her eyes, coursing down her cheeks, her hands useless at stemming the tide. 'It wasn't like that. I…I loved you.'

His fist smashed through the air, collided with his open palm with a crash. 'It was *exactly* like that! You wanted a rich husband. You got one. It was just bad luck for you that you picked the wrong one. And as for your so-called love, it proved to be as worthless as you.'

She heard a sound, a garbled cry, misery mixed with anguish, grief rent with despair, before realising it had emerged unbidden from the depths of her own agonising hopelessness.

He hated her. She knew he did. And she knew she deserved it. But she had not realised how deeply his hatred went, nor how much pain she had caused him.

In letting him go, in thinking she was setting him free by doing what she had, she might just as well have chained him to her betrayal.

But why could he not see that she was hurting as well? How could he have believed for a moment, let alone all these years, that she had never loved him? So she'd tried to be convincing in her rejection of him—she'd had to be—but didn't he know her better than that? Couldn't he see the lie she'd lived all these years?

Tears stung her eyes. She heard her name called behind her, but her feet kept pounding across the hot sands. She could not stay. Not like this. Not with him. Only apart could their wounds ever heal. Only apart was there a chance she might forget.

She was behind the wheel of one of the cars before anyone could stop her. The doors locked as she clutched hold of the steering wheel, feeling sick to her stomach as she looked down at the dashboard and its assortment of dials and gauges. Escape was suddenly more complicated, and she cursed Hussein for not letting her learn to drive. She'd had only two lessons before he'd discovered her secret. She squeezed her eyes shut, wishing as she'd wished a thousand times before that he'd had her beaten, instead of an innocent man, wishing that he'd hurt her rather than an innocent kitten. But hurting her had never been Hussein's way. Not physically, anyway.

Rafiq was shouting something, and she looked around through the haze of her tears to see him close, perilously close, the two drivers running behind, their arms flapping as uselessly as their white robes. Two driving lessons would have to be enough. She'd learned the basics in those. Start. Go. Stop. How difficult could it be?

She threw the car into 'drive' and pressed her foot hard down on the accelerator. It moved like a slug, and she slammed her fist against the steering wheel. 'Come on,' she urged, and floored her foot again, this time remembering the handbrake at the last moment. She jerked it up, releasing it, and the car lurched forward. She spun the wheel, spraying sand behind her in an arc, and took off in the direction the family had disappeared. She would catch up with them, plead with them to let her return to Shafar with them. It was not as if she was going to keep the car. The family had only just gone. They couldn't be too far ahead.

The vehicle snaked down the rutted track, difficult to follow and worse so through the blur of tears. He thought she'd married Hussein because she'd wanted a trophy husband? How could he think that, even if she *had* betrayed him? He should never have been there. Eleven months longer in the desert and he would probably have been over her. He wouldn't have cared so much that she'd gone. A year in the desert and he'd probably have grown out of her, been relieved she was no longer an issue for him on his return.

A fresh flood of tears followed that thought, refusing to be staunched. He should never have come back early from the desert! He should have stayed away. Then he wouldn't have seen her. And then she wouldn't have been forced to lie to him. Forced to try and prove it…

She sniffed. She'd played her hand too well and convinced him with her words and her actions that she'd never loved him. And somehow that had been the cruellest blow of all. For hadn't he seen her family gather around her, as if she was more a prisoner than a bride? Hadn't he witnessed his own father in the audience, smirking as his plans to rid himself of another woman unworthy of being his daughter-in-law had gone even better than he had expected?

A wail erupted from her throat, chopped up into sobs as the car bounced over the rutted track.

And hadn't he seen the sickness on her face at the reception, when Hussein had made her touch him—there—while Rafiq was watching?

How could he not have seen that? And he'd believed her lies, believed what his eyes had told him, and now he hated her. Damn him!

The car bounced and bucked its way along the desert track, past a sign that was behind her before she could read it, the wheel jerking out of her hands at times, the tyres finding it hard to get traction on the sandy hill. She couldn't remember a hill, but surely they had passed this way earlier, hadn't they?

All she could see through the mists of her vision was sand and more sand, red and endless, and if there were tyre-tracks anywhere the wind had long since blown them away.

Where was the track? Surely it was here somewhere. She blinked the tears from her eyes. Surely she hadn't lost it? Fear gripped her, and she pushed her foot harder down on the accelerator, desperate to get to the top of the dune so that she might get her bearings. But there was no stopping at the top of the rise. The tyres suddenly found purchase and the car roared up the slope, launching itself into space before crashing down on the other side in a crunch of springs and a grinding of metal. Pain blinded her as her head smashed against the door pillar, stunning her momentarily. The car was steering itself down the other side of the dune, half sliding, half careening, until the terrain thankfully flattened out, the car slowing as her foot slid from the accelerator.

Sera took a breath, blinked away her shock as she reclaimed control of the steering wheel. The side of her head throbbed where it had collided with the pillar, and she knew she'd have a headache later, but at least the shock had stopped the flow of tears and she could see where she was going. The dunes were lower here, with a wide, flat depression between. At last something was going right for her. This would definitely make for easier going until she regained the track.

She pressed down on the accelerator and the car surged over a last small dune. She was starting to relax, her racing heartbeat finally settling, when the car lurched, nose-first, its front wheels digging into the desert sands. She tried to power her way through, but the wheels spun uselessly, only digging themselves deeper. She battled with the gearstick, trying to coerce it into reverse gear, by chance happening on the button that allowed her to move it.

The tyres spun wildly in the other direction. Sera willed them to pull free of the clinging sands, and yet still the car refused to budge. If anything, it felt as if the car was burying itself still deeper.

Great. Her head sagged against her arms on the useless steering wheel and she felt despair welling up inside her once again. So much for escape. She was bogged down, stuck fast, up to her axles in sand in the middle of a desert, and she wasn't going anywhere until she dug herself out. *If* she could dig herself out. What a mess!

She pushed open her door to climb out and the car groaned and tilted, as if the weight of the open door had somehow pulled it over. It seemed to rock unsteadily for a moment then for a moment in which she wondered if she'd imagined the movement, and whether the knock on the head was affecting her balance, and then she saw it—the almost imperceptible movement in the sand below her, the slip and suck as it embraced the car's tyres and drew the car even deeper, the slow vortex that made clear its deadly mission.

And a new and chilling horror unfurled in her gut.

CHAPTER FIVE

HE WAS as angry as hell, and it wasn't all directed at the woman behind the wheel in the car ahead. Sand showered his windscreen, making it even harder to work out which way she was going. Who the hell had taught her to drive? She was all over the place, making no allowances for the rough terrain, least of all with the accelerator. Anyone would think the hounds of hell were after her.

He'd like to have a few words with the person who'd taught her to drive. Most of all, though, he was looking forward to having a few choice words with her. What the hell was she thinking, taking a car and driving off into the desert like that? What did she think it would solve?

Nothing.

All he'd done was deliver a few home truths and, like the spoilt society princess she was, she'd bolted. So maybe the truth hurt. Well, he had news for her: he had a few more home truths to get off his chest before their time together was over. And if she'd thought him angry before, she hadn't seen *anything* yet. Once he got her to stop he'd show her just how bad his temper could get.

She had that car all over the place, the vehicle bouncing and sliding from side to side, but it was when she suddenly veered off the rutted path and took off across the desert sands that fury turned to fear. He jerked the wheel around to follow, the heel of his hand hard against the horn, trying to get her attention, trying to warn her. But there was no stopping her, just as there had been no reasoning with her. She kept right on going.

What the hell was she thinking? She'd roared past a warning sign as if it had been nothing. But he'd seen the map. He'd seen the warning not to leave the road, and he'd seen the hatched areas that signalled the danger zone.

Sinking sands.

The desert around here was full of them, their appearance indistinguishable from the surrounding desert, traps for unwary travellers or wayward beasts.

He'd learned that lesson the hard way. He'd seen one swallow an entire camel during his month in the desert—the doomed animal's neck and head flailing hopelessly, its limbs already stuck deep within the remorseless sucking sand, its eyes wide and desperate, its panicked bleats sounding more like screams. The unnatural sound was what had drawn him to the pit's edge, and the noise had continued while he fought to save the doomed animal. But there had been no saving it, and soon, despite his efforts, both the camel and the sound had been swallowed up, and the desert had fallen silent but for the howl of the empty wind.

Oh, God, he'd seen first-hand what those sands could do.

The car in front screamed up a dune, launching itself into the hot, thin air, disappearing at a crazy angle over the other side and sending his gut lurching. He wanted her to stop—but not because she'd rolled the car!

It seemed to take an eternity to get there, until he topped the dune and could breathe a sigh of relief. He was in luck. She'd stopped at last. Maybe she'd come to her senses. Or maybe...

His blood chilled as he drew closer and skidded to a halt,

sending a cloud of red sand into the air. There was a reason she'd stopped. Her tyres were buried deep in sand, the car stuck fast.

And then he saw her door swing open and the car tilt ever so slightly with it, shifting ever deeper to one side, and something curdled in his gut.

'Sera, no!' he yelled. 'Don't get out!'

She turned her head, her eyes wide, but it was surprise he read in them first and foremost, as if she thought it odd that he should be here. What did she think? That he would let a lone woman drive off into the desert by herself? She didn't know him at all if she thought that.

'Stay there. Close the door.'

She looked at him as if he was mad, and he could understand why. She no doubt wanted to get out of the car, not lock herself inside while the car worked its way into a sandy grave. There was no point trying to explain to a society princess and no time, but the last thing he wanted was for the car to slip sideways and make it even harder for her to climb out.

Besides, it was a car and not a flailing-limbed camel, too panicked and too stupid to know that fighting the wet sand was the worst thing it could do and would only hasten its demise. The car would sink slower if it didn't go down nose first, but not with the doors open.

Maybe Sera was just too afraid to argue, because she reached out, trying to pull the heavy door back. 'It won't budge,' she cried, and he cursed when he saw why.

Already the bottom corner of the door was dragging at the sucking sands. Soon the soft sand would pour through the open door, claiming the car for its own. 'Leave it,' he ordered, 'and get into the back.'

The car tilted further as she scrambled over the front seats. Meanwhile he moved cautiously closer, testing each step before giving it his full weight. 'Watch out!' he heard her call, as if he were the one stuck in the middle of a pit of sinking sand.

His foot found the edge of the pit, sinking into the soft, damp sand just a couple of feet short of the car's tailgate, but at least she hadn't landed the car any further in. He might have to congratulate her for that once they were out. Still, it would be a stretch, but he should be able to reach the tailgate. He made sure both his feet were on solid sand and then leaned over, letting himself fall the last few inches to the doors, wrenching the handle, fighting the angle of the sinking car to pull the back doors open.

'I'm sorry,' she cried, from where she sat huddled in the back seat. 'But I couldn't stay back there. I had to get away.'

The car slipped deeper then, tilting further, the metal groaning an unearthly groan, metal and rubber against the sucking forces of sand, and she winced, her fingers clutching the back seat like claws. The acid reply that he'd been so ready to let fly from his lips died a rapid death. 'Forget it,' he simply said, pulling stuff out of the back of the car and tossing it behind him, hoping it reached solid ground but more intent on making space right now for her to climb through. 'Just be ready to jump over when I tell you.' He found a folded tarpaulin and flapped it open with one hand, spreading it out on the soft ground below him as best he could. It wasn't much, but at least it would be some protection if anything they needed fell in his rush to clear space.

'I'm sorry about the car,' she babbled. 'I didn't know.'

'I said forget it!' He did a rapid assessment and decided he'd made enough space for her to climb through. 'Now, let's get you out of there. Are you ready?'

She nodded uncertainly and he leaned out of the way to give her more room. She hauled up her robe to clamber inelegantly over the tilted seat, revealing a long sweep of golden skin followed by another just as perfect, just as lean and smooth and long, distracting him when he least needed a distraction.

The car dipped sideways into the sand and his hold slipped with it. 'Rafiq!' Sera screamed, reaching for him as he fell, but he had landed on the tarpaulin, his weight spread, and was able to roll away and be on firm sand again before he could sink.

'Now, get ready,' he told her, relieved to see she had tucked the offending legs back under her robe, where they could not distract him again. 'Reach for my hand, and when I give the word, you jump. Got that?'

She nodded and dragged in a breath, as if steeling herself, her eyes a mixture of fear and apprehension.

He leaned out towards her and she balanced as best she could in the sloping doorway, reaching out her own hand to him. His fingers curled hungrily around her small hand even as the car pitched nose-down, with sand pouring into the front seat. Sera gasped, lifted higher with the back of the car, her fingers slipping from his as her arm stretched. But his grip only tightened. There was no way he was letting her go.

'Now!'

She sprang at his command, the same instant as he pulled on her hand, launching her across the distance with so much force that she collided against his chest. His arms immediately wrapped around her as he spun her away from the edge of the pit and to safety.

'What the hell were you thinking?' he yelled. 'What the hell were you playing at?'

And her response came not with words but as tremors. They started out as a shiver that set her body quaking in his arms. He looked down at her flustered face, at the black-as-night eyes that looked up at him, eyes wounded by the verbal attack that had come so close on the heels of her rescue, and he looked at the open mouth as she dragged in air, at those lips, so close to him now that their proximity must surely equate with possession.

Possession he had no choice but to take.

His mouth crashed down upon hers in a brutal kiss, a kiss that he tore from her, a kiss that spoke of dread and fear and loss, of agony and relief as his mouth plundered hers, his hands sliding up her slim back to bury themselves in that silken curtain of black hair and anchor her close to him. Remorseless and ruthless. Avenging himself for the wrongs of the past. Like a man dying of thirst, he drank deeply of that first heady stream. Unable to stop even when good sense dictated he should, even when he knew his life depended on restraint.

There was no restraint here.

Instead, all the things he felt, all the things he'd wanted to say to her in the past years, all the strain of the last few short hours—everything spilled out into that kiss as his mouth savaged hers while they stood amidst the sandy dunes under a scorching desert sun.

Until she flinched, and his hand in her hair came away sticky and damp.

Breathless and conflicted, searching for answers to questions he didn't understand and finding none, he pushed her away from him as abruptly as he'd pulled her into his kiss, his chest labouring, his senses shot as he tried to make sense of the discovery.

He looked down at his fingertips, felt something twisting and curling inside him. 'You're bleeding.'

Somehow Sera managed to keep upright, although her legs felt boneless, her senses in a shambles. He'd been angry with her, hadn't he? So angry after he'd pulled her out of the car. But then he'd kissed her—a kiss that had knocked her remaining breath clean out of her lungs and left her more confused than ever.

And all he could worry about was a bang on the head she'd forgotten completely in the thunderclap of a kiss that had blanked her mind, wiping clear the terror of her escape, the relief at being safe, the fact that he hated her.

He hated her. He'd told her so. He'd shown her in his words and his actions.

So why had he just kissed her?

'Your Highness!' The breathless cry came from the dunes behind and she turned her head to see one of the drivers, half jogging, half stumbling through the sand, his face red and sweat streaked from his exertions, his white robe sticking to him and stained with sand. The other followed a few paces behind, looking no less stressed, and guilt sliced into her as cleanly as a surgeon's scalpel.

She was the cause of their distress. And their concern for their prince meant they must follow even as he chased the crazy woman in the car. Rafiq would not have thought of such things—he had been so many years in Australia that he would not understand the depth of their responsibility to a member of their royal family. But she knew how the palace worked. And she should have realised Rafiq would follow. He probably hadn't finished telling her how little he thought of her—for that reason alone he would have been driven to pursue her.

But out here, deep in the desert, when she hadn't cared what might happen to her, she should at least have realised how dangerous her actions were for everyone else.

When had she become so selfish? She had not thought through her actions. She had not thought of anyone else at all.

But of course the men did not take issue with her—it was not their place to judge. Instead, both men stared at the doomed car, now sinking its way deeper into the desert itself, offering prayers of thanks for their prince's safekeeping as they neared.

'Your Highness,' one of them panted, his hand over his chest as he dipped his head with respect. 'We feared for your safety.' His eyes were once more drawn to the bizarre sight of the doomed vehicle, and he caught his breath before he could continue. 'Are you all right?'

'I'm fine,' Rafiq said, handing water to the men. 'Drink. Then one of you see to Sera. She has a wound on her head. The other one, help me. The car is beyond winching now, but there's still time to save a few more things.'

In a daze, Sera allowed herself to be guided to the blissfully cool air-conditioned car, where the first aid kit was accessed. 'I'm sorry to cause so much trouble,' she said to the man as he tended her wound, but he merely shrugged philosophically, as if there was nothing unusual in a woman going crazy and causing mayhem in the desert.

Her actions had lost them a vehicle.

She'd lost them hours of daylight.

And somewhere along the line she seemed to have lost a grip on herself.

It must be a kind of crazy, she thought, wincing as his fingers prodded at her head. A few short hours ago she'd been perfectly content with her life, or at least as content as someone with her past could hope to be. She had a role at the palace with a woman who understood, and she performed her duties well. She was quiet. Thoughtful. Responsible.

Until Rafiq had returned and her world had been turned upside down. Who was she that she could forget who she was so easily? That she could be swept away on this unfamiliar tidal rush of memories and emotion?

She squinted past her carer to where Rafiq was bundling the goods he'd salvaged from the car before she'd jumped. His pale shirt and trousers were smudged with sand, tendrils of his dark hair clung damp against his brow and his features were set. Even under the hot sun, his eyes had returned to their glacial blue.

They hadn't looked cold before.

He'd held her in his arms and looked down at her and her

heart had skipped a beat. For his blue eyes had simmered with heat, a boiling spring steaming with desire, a summer storm that promised lightning set to rent the sky in two. And then his desperate eyes had found her mouth and her trembling had changed direction. She had trembled not from the shock of the near disaster; she had trembled from the shock of knowing he wanted her.

And from the shock of wanting him.

Her hands twisted into knots in her lap. *She must be crazy to even think it.*

And yet there had been no mistaking Rafiq's desire. She had witnessed the need in his storm-tossed eyes. And while it had shocked her, and sent her trembling anew, she could not deny that the knowledge had secretly thrilled her, even while it had terrified her.

Rafiq still wanting her?

It was beyond comprehension. Beyond belief.

Even his kiss made no sense. For his kiss, when it had come, as his turbulent eyes had promised it must, had been nothing like the tender kisses they'd exchanged in their youth. This kiss had been ruthless and hard, savage in its intent, almost as if he'd wanted to punish her, and yet still it had brought with it an awakening of her senses, an unfurling of emotions and passions that she'd been long since denied.

Had long since denied herself.

A kiss so momentous it had reawakened both her heart and her soul.

But at what cost?

Her hands twisted and retwisted while she sat patiently, an expression of the turmoil going on inside herself, until the driver pronounced his work done. A graze and a bruise was the only visible external damage, but he gave her a warning to let him know if her pain worsened.

Could her pain worsen? Surely it wasn't possible. For this pain she felt now, the pain uppermost and foremost in her mind, was not just the mere throb of a temple; this pain was akin to the intense sting of a numbed limb whose blood supply had been cut off and then suddenly resumed, whose numb flesh had reawakened to the stabbing pins and needles of sensation as the flow returned.

Except that pain did not normally last longer than a minute or two, and this was not some arm or leg that felt the pain of sensation returning.

This was her heart.

Their party made camp where the desert track met the sea. The sun was already low on its downward track towards the water, a fireball already sinking, almost extinguished, and the mountains that were their goal loomed dark and threatening before them.

Rafiq had not been happy, but there was nothing else for it. In the light of the advice from the travellers at the oasis, and supported by his drivers, Rafiq had agreed that they had lost too much time today, and that the path up to Marrash would be too treacherous in the dark. They would camp by the coast.

And while he didn't say it outright, while the drivers remained silent on the subject, Sera knew he held her responsible. Knew that he was angry.

For, when once his eyes had all but demanded her attention, he'd been avoiding her ever since the accident, ensuring he sat in the front with one driver while she sat in the back seat with the other, guaranteeing they wouldn't have to share the same seat or inadvertently make eye contact. Guaranteeing he wouldn't have to so much as look at her.

Even now, while the camp buzzed with activity around them, while a meal was prepared and the final touches put to the tents that would house them tonight, he kept his distance, leaving her to her own devices.

How could he make any plainer the fact that he regretted their kiss? And how could he have better shown his contempt for her but to bend her to his will and then drop her cold?

Which didn't make forgetting it any easier for her.

For his taste lingered on her lips.

And the memory of the touch of his fingers raking through her hair while his mouth had plundered hers still set her scalp to tingling. How was she expected to just forget those sensations? That kiss had awakened something inside her. A yearning. Long-forgotten feelings.

She swallowed, squeezed her eyes shut, and wished she could so easily shut out the tangle of unwanted emotions. Because she didn't want to feel. She had taught herself long ago not to feel. It was the only way she'd been able to close out the revulsion. The disgust.

And yet his kiss had brought feeling back, sharp and prickling and uncomfortable.

Later, after a meal heavy with silence, she wandered alone along the long sweep of sandy beach, the caw of gulls and the foaming crash of the waves and the sea-softened wind that toyed with her hair her only companions.

Her feet left imprints in the damp sand, footprints the next incoming swoosh of wave wiped away, as if she'd never walked that way.

On and on she walked, until the lure of the beckoning sea became too much, and she stopped and decided she was far enough away from the camp. She walked higher up the shore, to where the foaming waves would not reach, and stood there, contemplating the endless sea, shimmering silver under the moon's pearlescent glow.

The tug of the water and the promise of the ocean's soothing caress became too much, and she picked up her hem and scooped her bulky *abaya* over her head, shaking her long hair free as she dropped the garment to the sand.

She strode into the welcoming water, felt the refreshing rush as a wave came to greet her, then the suck as it receded, coaxing her deeper. She waded in until she was waist-deep and then dived under an incoming wave, setting her nerve-endings alight with the sensual slip of water against skin.

He hadn't really believed she'd been running away. He didn't really believe she'd try anything like that again. But that didn't mean he didn't think she was an accident waiting to happen. Just a short walk, she'd said after their meal, to clear her head—and yet already she'd walked the length of the beach and then some before she'd finally stopped. He'd wondered if he should turn, or just wait for her there in the dark. She was bound to be unimpressed if she learned he'd followed her.

And then she'd done the unexpected and pulled her dress up and over her head, and the air had been punched from his lungs.

In the light of the moon her skin glowed gold, her hair shining black, tumbling down to her slim waist as she shook it free from her dress. Long-limbed, and with curves where they should be, she stood under the moonlight like a golden goddess, before she moved to meet the water, her hips swaying, her long hair rippling down her back, as graceful and elegant as a water bird.

Sera.

His Sera.

CHAPTER SIX

NEED punched into him like a curled fist. It had hit him hard the first time, when he had kissed her in the desert after pulling her to her escape. Hit him unexpectedly, with its force and sheer ferocity. Because he'd realised finally that his kiss hadn't just been about vengeance. It had been need that had driven him to taste her lips. Need that had made him crush her to him as if he'd never let her go again.

A need that had rocked him to the core when he had put her away from him, determined to keep her at arm's length, where the siren could no more mess with his head.

But now, seeing her like this, golden-skinned and lithe, and with the water slipping its cool magic up her silken thighs, it was as if his need had taken root and become a living thing.

How could one be jealous of the water in the sea? But right now he was. He wanted to be there in place of it, caressing the secret places he never had, sliding past that silken skin, holding her flesh in his thrall.

Why shouldn't he have her?

She was nothing to him now but a dark memory. Nothing but an itch that had never been scratched. Once upon a time he'd respected her innocence, had been prepared to wait until the right moment, until the ceremony that would see them tied together for ever. But why should he wait now? There was nothing left to wait for. There would be no ceremony, no forever, and she was a widow, no longer the innocent.

Why shouldn't he have her?

She hadn't fought against his kiss. Even if she had not wanted it, as he himself had not, she had not protested or struggled to be free. Instead her body had swayed into his, melted against his, her mouth opening at his invitation just as surely as he knew her body would open for him. After all, she was a woman now practised in such moves.

What was one more man to her now?

He wandered closer to where she'd left her *abaya*, crumpled on the sand, and dropped the sandals he'd been carrying in his hands. Out in the sea she was diving through the waves like a dolphin, her body sleek, her back curved, the moonlight turning her body to a swish of silk through the water. He envied the black hair that hugged her skin and curved around her breasts just as he envied the sea that embraced her.

She was beautiful. A goddess. And he wanted her.

She should have been his a long time ago.

She could be his now.

And he would have her.

Sera wanted to stay there for ever, but she knew that she had already been away too long, that her presence would be missed and that Rafiq had probably sent out a search party.

Besides, the water had not numbed her heated skin as she needed. Instead the waves had been a sensual massage against her skin, its motion past her skin feeding the tension that had beset her body ever since Rafiq had appeared outside his mother's apartment, the remorseless tension that had cranked up one-hundredfold when he'd folded her so tightly in his arms and kissed her senseless.

She shivered in the water, suddenly feeling cold, and turned for shore, catching a wave and riding it into the shore, where she stood in the shallows, put her arms behind her head to squeeze the water from her hair, and looked up the beach for the place where she had left her gown.

The tremor squeezed every muscle tight when she found it, and she dropped her arms and crossed them defensively across her belly when she saw who was sitting beside it.

Rafiq.

How long had he been sitting there, lounging back against the sand like a modern-day pirate, his white shirt bright in the moonlight, his pants rolled up at the ankles? How long had he been watching her?

What defences the sea had managed to wash away were hastily re-erected. The relaxing benefits of the motion of the waves were suddenly for naught. With her water-cooled flesh exposed to both the balmy breeze and to his gaze, her flesh was turning to goosebumps.

Couldn't he at least look away?

She forced herself forward, crossing the sand on uncertain legs, refusing to meet his gaze, wishing she'd thought to pack a swimsuit in her hastily packed bag. She made a swipe for her *abaya*, but he got there first, picking it up in his hands, resting his elbows on his knees as he held the garment. But at least he wasn't looking at her any more. His gaze was turned out to sea, no doubt so that he could pretend he hadn't noticed she had just been reaching for it.

'Have a nice swim?' he asked, the sides of his mouth turned up.

He dared to smile? As if this was some kind of game? 'What are you doing here?'

'Don't you know it's dangerous to swim alone at night?'

'Don't you know it's rude to spy on people?' The words were

out before she could stop them, her boldness shocking her so much that she took an involuntary step back across the sand in defence. She wasn't used to thinking such thoughts any more, let alone speaking them aloud—not when she knew what the consequences could be.

But Rafiq's smile merely widened, as if he hadn't noticed her transgression. He kept his gaze seawards. 'I was worried about you.'

'You thought I'd run away?'

'Not really. But you do have this thing with sand. I didn't want to take any chances.'

Was that supposed to be funny? Or her cue to fall down and thank him for rescuing her today, even when he'd frozen her out and treated her as if she didn't exist ever since he'd rescued her? When he'd snatched up her clothes so she couldn't get dressed? Not a chance.

'As you can see, I'm fine.'

Now he did look at her, his eyes searing a path all the way from her knees to her face, the slow way, until her skin burned and she cursed herself for inviting him to look.

'Would you mind handing me my dress?'

His white teeth flashed in the moonlight. 'What if I said I liked the view just the way it is?'

It wasn't what she wanted to hear, but even while her flesh tingled a tiny part of her wanted to rejoice in his words, because it had been Rafiq himself who had uttered them. But it was still wrong—for so many, many reasons. He shouldn't look at her that way. Couldn't he see her shame? Couldn't he tell?

She remembered the men who had admired her body and her looks, the men who had run their pudgy fingers through her hair, their alcohol-heavy breath perilously close to her own as they had whispered secret wishes in her ear that had turned her stomach.

And she remembered too the men who had recoiled from

her, their faces shocked and appalled, as if she were no more than a piece of dirt.

She was worthless. Could he not tell?

She spun around on the soft sand, banishing the poisonous memories as she turned her back on Rafiq for evoking the twisted memories of days thankfully gone, for the long-forgotten desires of her own wayward body combining inside her into a potent mix. 'I just wanted to have a swim in private. Is that too much to ask?'

And something in her tone must have worked its way into his arrogant brain, for suddenly he was next to her, holding out her *abaya*. She snatched it from his hands, bundling it over her head and punching through her arms, struggling to get it down over her still-damp body, not waiting to get it right down over her legs before she set off down the beach, away from him, desperate now to return to the camp where there were others, where there could not be this talk of 'liking the view' of her, undressed or otherwise. Where the conversation would be on safer territory and not in this permanent quicksand that seemed to surround their every exchange.

She sighed. She'd hoped earlier that she'd had her last encounter with the sinking sands, and yet they were all around her, in his words and in his heated looks, ready to trap her and suck her down.

'I don't need you to follow me,' she protested, enjoying her newfound freedom to speak her mind as he drew level alongside her. 'I don't want you here now.'

'You are a woman walking in the dark alone. Your safety is my responsibility.'

'This is Qusay. It is safe for women here.'

'There are still strangers. Tourists.'

Ridiculous! There was no one else here in this remote corner of their country. The roads were too basic, the infrastructure negligible, and the closest this part of the coast had to a tourist resort were the tiny villages that scraped an existence from the sea and he knew it. But there was a better way of showing how flawed his argument was. 'Are not you a tourist yourself? Should I then be fearful of you?'

His intake of air was audible, and his already gravel-rich voice deepened. 'I am Qusani, born and bred.'

'But you don't live here. You're only here until Kareef is crowned, and then you'll return to your home halfway around the world. That makes you little more than a tourist. And, based on your own assertion, that makes you someone I should be wary of. Given the way you snatched up my *abaya* so I could not cover my body, I'd say you were right.'

He grabbed her arm, his fingers like a manacle around her, wheeling her around. Her eyes widened with something that looked more like fear than the surprise he'd anticipated. Only there was no time to try to work out why—not when he had a point to make. 'I am not a tourist! What the hell is wrong with you? I am Prince of Qusay.'

She blinked, and when she reopened her eyes the fear had gone, but there was a brightness there that he hadn't noticed before. A life force that had been missing. 'So they say,' she whispered, soft as the silken sands on which they stood. 'But are you really? Why is it that you cannot even look like a prince of Qusay?' She waved her free hand towards him. 'Look at what you wear. Armani suits. Cotton shirts with collars. This is not the Qusani way. Why do you insist on turning your back on your heritage if you are so proud to be Qusani?'

'Because this is not my home!'

And she smiled, and thanked the force that had released her from having to hold her tongue every second of every day, even if that force had a little too much to do with Rafiq's unwanted kiss.

'Exactly my point. A tourist. In which case, I'd better get back to camp before I put myself in any more danger.'

Breathless and heady, she jerked her arm out of his hand and strode off down the beach, expecting any moment for him to run after her and grab her again, to show her how wrong she was. But there was no thud of footsteps across the sand behind her and no iron-fingered clasp to stop her.

Rafiq watched her walk away, wanting to growl, wanting to argue, wanting to protest. A tourist she'd likened him to. A mere holidaymaker who had no right to be here in Qusay.

Yet those protests died, his words stymied, as he remembered. She'd smiled. Maybe at him rather than with him, but she'd actually smiled. And didn't that turn his growl of irritation into a growl of something infinitely more satisfying?

He turned to watch her go, hypnotised by the sway of her hips under the *abaya* that now clung to her sea-moistened curves. Curves that he had seen in close proximity. Curves that he had ached to reach his hands out to—curves he could have reached out for if only they hadn't been filled with the fabric of her dress.

A siren he'd thought her before. A sea witch who lured men to their deaths.

Maybe so—but not before he'd had her first.

She was lucky to have escaped him this time. Even now he should be tumbling her down on the soft sand, rolling her under him, instead of watching her march alone up the beach like a victor.

But then she'd changed. He snatched up the sandals he'd left where he'd sat waiting for her, meaning to turn and follow Sera, but stopped, dropping down onto the sand instead, wondering at this new revelation.

She *had* changed. The woman he'd seen outside his mother's apartments—the woman who'd refused to look at him let alone speak to him, the woman whose eyes were bleak and filled with despair, the woman he'd barely recognised as the Sera he'd known—was gone.

A new Sera seemed to have taken her place. Not his old Sera, for the Sera he remembered had been sweet and filled with light and laughter. The Sera who was emerging from that bleak shell was different. Tougher underneath. And yet with such an air of fragility, as if at any moment she might shatter into a thousand pieces. But at last she'd smiled.

A tourist, she'd called him, challenging him to deny it, refusing to accept his arguments when he had offered them.

Was that how he was seen? Rafiq the tourist prince?

The idea grated, even as he could see some kind of case for it. For what thought had he really given to Qusay? No more than he'd ever given it before—it was the island of his birth, and the place that had let him down. The place he'd ultimately turned his back on. He hadn't considered what it would mean to be its prince, even while his own brother was about to be crowned.

Instead he'd put his homeland behind him a very long time ago. Self-defence, he knew, because the best times in his life had not been with his brothers or with their domineering father, but with a black-haired girl who had seemed like an extension of himself, who had been the light of his life.

No, he knew that if he had thought of Qusay at all it would only have brought back memories of Sera, and he'd had no intention of inflicting that upon himself.

So much for being a prince of Qusay. What did he really know of this land, when he had abandoned his existing responsibilities and his links so readily?

The moon provided no answers, and the dark sea refused to come to his rescue.

Could Sera be right? he wondered, as he set off back towards camp long after she had departed. He *was* little more than a tourist here. An accident of birth might have made him their prince, he might be ruler of a business empire of his own making, but there was precious little else to commend him.

It was just lucky he was not the eldest. Kareef would make a good king. A just king. Kareef would be the king Qusay needed.

Sleep eluded Rafiq in his tent that night, no matter his recent long journey, the comfy wide bed with plush pillows and comforter, and the otherwise relaxing sound of the waves crashing in, wave after endless wave, rolling in along the shore. But Rafiq did not mind the sleepless hours. Because when he did sleep it was his own private agony, and his dreams were filled with the song of sirens, of a beauty once forbidden to him, of a beauty that still called to him.

It was hard enough not to think of her when he was awake—impossible not to remember her long-limbed perfection as she'd risen from the sea, the water streaming from her golden body. And when he slept his dreams were owned by her, closeted away under the curtain of her thick black hair—the hair he'd once buried his whispers in, the hair he'd worn heavy across his chest as she'd laid her head upon his shoulder.

He jerked awake suddenly, certain he could smell the herb-rinsed scent of her hair on his pillow. But he flopped back down alone, strangely disappointed, his breathing ragged as the spindly fingers of dawn squeezed their way through the tiny gaps in his tent.

What the hell was wrong with him?

The mountain road was in no better state than reported—no more than single lane in many places, with mountain slippages making it even more risky in others. Below them as they rose up the twisted road, the endless desert rolled on. Somewhere out there was Shafar, Sera reflected, and the palace. Soon

Kareef would be crowned, and Rafiq would return to his other world, and things would return to some kind of normality.

She could hardly wait.

And then she glanced across at Rafiq, sitting alongside the driver in the front seat, and thought, *liar*.

For, while she wished he'd never bothered to turn up for his brother's coronation, and as much as she wished to get her emotions back under control, seeing him go, watching him leave again after he'd reawakened feelings that should have been left dormant, would be devastating.

He looked over his shoulder then, snaring her gaze. Questions swirled in his own blue depths before she could turn her head away, her skin tingling under her *abaya*, her breasts suddenly sensitive and full. It hurt, this sudden reawakening of her senses. It stung physically and mentally.

She closed her eyes, feigning sleep, trying to block out both him and the uncomfortable sensations, trying to cut the invisible tie that seemed to bind them even now, after so many empty years.

But when she gave up on the pretence and opened them again he was still studying her, his eyes steel-blue with intent, and her body shuddered anew. Spot fires were starting under her skin, their flames licking secret places, building secret needs that made her more ashamed of her body than ever. Evidence, if she'd needed anything more, that her body welcomed his attentions and would miss him when he was gone.

Evidence that the sooner he left, the better.

The vehicle rattled and bumped up the steep escarpment. Their ascent up the mountainous path was seeming to take for ever, although it was at most a couple of hours. Finally the narrow track opened out, widening where the land levelled between two craggy mountain peaks, and stunted trees and bushes clung to the roadside. Buildings appeared, low and squat—mud brick buildings made from the same red cliffs of the mountains.

They had reached Marrash. Goats brayed where they were tethered at the sides of the road, and children gathered in groups under the shade of spindly trees, jumping up and shouting as they approached, as if the arrival of visitors was a rare treat. Given the state of the one road leading into it, it probably was.

Rafiq surveyed the town suspiciously. *This* was the place where a fabric of such beauty had been created? In this dry and dusty mountain village? It hardly seemed possible.

Had his mother sent him on a wild goose chase? And, if so, for what purpose? And then a movement behind him caught his eye, a flash of black as Sera lifted her hand to shade her eyes as she looked out of her window.

And he remembered her moonlit skin as she'd emerged from the water, a goddess from the sea, and he didn't care if it was a wild goose chase, because it had given him the chance to even the score with Sera. If he was going to lose sleep, he might as well be better occupied than spending the hours in tortured and fractured rest.

Last night she'd thrown him with her accusations of being a tourist prince. Last night he'd let her go.

He wouldn't let her go again.

He *was* a prince, whether she liked it or not. And, just as he'd set himself the task of making a business success of himself, so too would he be a success in his role as prince.

And when it came to dealing with Sera he was the one who would set down the ground rules.

The car came to a stop in a largish square in the centre of the village, with the dusty squeak of brakes and the sound of the children laughing and calling as they swarmed around the car.

Soon the square was filled, as people emerged from their houses, squinting against the bright daylight, smiles lighting up their faces. A white-haired man came forward, his spine bent, his skin tanned like leather, the lines on his face deep like the crevasses of the very mountains themselves.

'Your Highness,' he said, bowing low as Rafiq emerged from the car. 'It is indeed a pleasure to have you visit our humble village. I am Suleman, the most senior of our village elders. You have come to see our treasures, I believe? Come, take refreshment, and then it will be our pleasure to show you those things of which Marrash is justifiably proud.'

So there were treasures to be seen after all? Rafiq followed the elder, and the small party made its way through the crowded square. Wide-eyed children reached out to touch him, and women holding babies asked for his blessing as he passed, or sent their blessings to Kareef for his upcoming coronation.

How many hands he held, how many babies' cheeks he touched and murmured soft words to he quickly lost count— but he could not forget Sera's accusation of last night.

Tourist prince.

She would pay for that.

CHAPTER SEVEN

RAFIQ was impatient. He had two priorities now. Seal the deal with the Marrashis, if there was to be one, and bed Sera. But the second could not happen until the first was completed, and so far he hadn't seen any treasures. Instead the rounds of coffee seemed endless, the plates of tiny treats never-ending—as if they had all the time in the world to engage in polite conversation with the dozen elders of the village, about everything but the reason they'd come.

After ten years building his empire in Australia, he was frustrated. This was not the way he did business. But he was in Qusay, and things were done differently here. Time seemed to pass more slowly, formalities had to be observed, niceties endured.

And so he observed and endured and smiled through gritted teeth, and made a note to thank his buyers, who did this all the time in order to source the goods for his emporiums. They must have patience in abundance.

Sera, he noticed with mounting irritation, looked like patience personified. She sat elegantly, her feet tucked out of sight underneath her, her back straight and her attention one hundred percent on whoever was speaking.

Or maybe not quite one hundred per cent.

For the second time he caught the slide of her eyes towards

him, the panicked flight when she saw she'd been caught, the colour that tinted her smooth-skinned cheeks.

It was all he could do to drag his attention back to the ceremony.

Finally, with the last question as to the health of his brother and his mother answered, the coffee pot withdrawn, Suleman appeared satisfied. 'Now,' he said, his eyes lighting up like one about to bestow a special gift on a child, 'shall I show you our treasures?'

Rafiq smiled and nodded. *At last.* If there was little to see they could be out of here and back in Shafar in plenty of time for tonight's state banquet. He stepped back to allow Sera to precede him as Suleman led the way, and breathed in the scent of her hair, remembering a golden goddess emerging from the sea.

Although there was something to be said for staying one more night in the camp by the sea.

The palace would be crowded with visitors arriving for the coronation, noisy and demanding, and it would be near impossible to lever Sera from his mother's apartments even if there were somewhere private to take her.

Whereas at the camp by the sea they would be practically alone.

A deep breath saw oxygen-rich blood jump to the ready, like an army eager to do battle.

There was no rush to leave.

It was perfect.

Suleman led them out into the street again, and onto a narrow path that ran along a thin stream. Fed by a spring, Suleman told them, a gift from the gods. Instantly it felt cooler, the path lined with grasses and shaded by trees. There was a grove of orange trees too, the tang of citrus on the air.

The path led them past a tiny shop, selling everything from rugs to lace to knick-knacks, where an old woman sat in a chair in front, fanning her face. She broke into a big gappy smile when she saw Rafiq, swinging herself up onto her bowed legs.

'Prince Rafiq,' she cried, her voice frail and thin—and how she even saw him, let alone recognised him with the cataracts clouding her eyes and turning her lenses almost white, was a miracle. He went to greet her, and she pressed his hand between her bony, surprisingly strong hands. 'Please, have something from my shop.'

Suleman stood behind them patiently, his fingers laced in front of him, while Sera could not resist looking closer at the table laden with trinkets set amongst tiny lamps and coffee pots. She picked up one of the lamps, the chips of green stuck to the brass twinkling in the dappled light.

'This is beautiful,' she told the woman. And then to Rafiq, 'Your mother would love this.'

'How much is it?' he asked, reaching into his pockets.

'Take it for the Sheikha!' the old woman insisted, picking up another, larger and more resplendent in its decoration. 'And one for Prince Kareef, to celebrate the upcoming celebrations— a gift from Abizah of Marrash.'

He wanted to argue the point—clearly the woman was scraping out an existence without giving away her stock—but she was already reaching for paper to wrap the gifts, pressing them into his hands when she was finished.

'And now something for your beautiful wife…' Her hand hovered over the table of wares.

Rafiq coughed. Sera at his side bowed her head, her face suddenly colouring. 'Sera is the Sheikha's companion,' he corrected, as gently as he could.

'Yes, yes,' the old woman said, waving one hand and taking no notice. 'For now, perhaps, yes. Aha!' Her hand scooped up the prize—a choker Sera hadn't noticed behind all the other trinkets, made up of clusters of the same green chips that had adorned the fabric she'd fetched for the Sheikha, the same green chips that shone on the tiny lamp, but these chips were threaded on gold thread, with trails of the tiny gems hanging from it in a wide V-shape. Sera gasped. It was divine. A work of art.

'It is too much!' Sera protested. 'I cannot accept such a gift from you.'

The old woman brushed her concerns aside with a sweep of one hand. 'Nonsense.' She passed the necklace to Rafiq. 'Put this on your wife. My eyes and fingers are not as good as once they were.'

He held the ends of the sparkling necklace in each hand, not even bothering to correct her this time, still rattled by her earlier words and not sure she would listen anyway. 'Turn around,' he told her, and saw Sera's slight shake of her head, her dark eyes helpless, deep velvet pools. But dutifully she turned. He put his arms over her head, dropping the necklace onto the skin of her throat. There was a pulse beating there, urgent, bewitching, and he had the insane desire to press his mouth to it and feel her very life force beneath his lips.

As if she read his thoughts, he felt her breath hitch, her chest rising with it.

He drew back, enclosed the golden chain around her hair, fastened the closure.

He could have left it at that. Stepped away and let her free her hair from the circle of the chain. But he could not.

Instead he slid his hands under her heavy black hair, like silk in his hands as he lifted its weight, feeling the tremors slide through her as the backs of his fingers skimmed her neck.

And again he could have left it at that.

But still he could not walk away. Not until he had smoothed her hair down—hair that was a magnet for his fingers, hair that he wanted to bury his face in so he might drink in more of the scent of herbs and flowers.

The old woman handed him a mirror, and reluctantly he had no choice but to take it. 'Take a look,' he invited, his hand on

Sera's shoulder as she slowly turned. Against her golden skin the emerald chips winked and sparkled, the perfect foil for her dark eyes and black hair.

Colour, he realised. That was what she needed. Colour to accentuate her dark beauty, not bury it under so much black. 'You look beautiful,' he said, not sure whether he should have said *it* looks beautiful, suddenly not certain which he meant.

Sera gasped when she looked in the mirror. 'It is exquisite. But, please, you must let me pay for it.'

The old woman nodded and smiled. 'You may pay me with your smile—it is all that I ask. For one so beautiful should not be sad. Listen to Abizah, for she knows these things. Soon you will find your happiness.' And in the next instant she was waving them away, as if they were keeping her from other customers, of which there were none. 'Now, you who could be King, be away on your business, and thank you,' she said, bowing, as if he'd just done her the favour of her life. 'Thank you for stopping at my shop.'

'She is a generous woman,' Rafiq said to Suleman, and he smiled indulgently as they continued along the path.

'Abizah is Marrash's wise woman. Her eyes are not so good, as she says, yet still she sees things.'

'What kind of things?' asked Sera.

'The future, some say.' And then he shrugged. 'But others believe she speaks nothing but nonsense. Sometimes it can be one and the same. Come this way; the factory is waiting for us.'

The future? Rafiq wondered. Or nonsense?

Why had she addressed him as 'you who *could* be King'? Did she mean if not for Kareef? It seemed a strange way to refer to him.

But not half as strange as it had felt when she had called Sera his wife. Even after his correction still she'd persisted, half the time speaking in riddles. No wonder some said she spoke nonsense!

* * *

Sera put a hand to her throat, where the tiny stones of the choker lay cool and smooth against her flesh. She was still trembling, although whether from the words of the old woman or as a result of Rafiq's sensual touch and the fan of his warm breath against her throat, she wasn't sure.

Why should she feel so much now, when she had felt nothing for so long? Why had feelings come back to life, turning everything into colour instead of black and white?

And why had the old woman assumed she was Rafiq's wife? They were travelling together, it was true, and Rafiq might not be as well known to the Qusanis as his brother Kareef. But she had persisted even after Rafiq's gentle attempt to correct her. And what had she meant about Sera being the Sheikha's companion 'for now'?

Despite the warmth of the day, Sera shivered as she followed their guide, haunted by Abizah's words, trying to make sense of them. How did the old woman know she'd not been happy for a long time? Had she found it written on her face, or guessed it from the black robes she favoured? But how could she have known when she was nearly blind?

Whatever, the encounter with the old woman had shaken her, and the magnitude of the gift she'd bestowed upon her was unsettling. Even though of polished emerald chips rather than cut stones, the necklace was such a beautiful thing, the craftsmanship superb. How could she ever repay her?

In a momentary pause in their guide's monologue, she touched a hand to Rafiq's arm. 'There must be something we can do to repay her. There must be.' And Rafiq's eyes turned from what had looked like shock at her touch to understanding, and without his saying a word she somehow knew he understood.

The path had widened to a courtyard, and a squat, long

building that seemed to disappear into the very mountain peak behind, its timber door knotted and pitted with age. Suleman stood before it, his hand on the latch.

'Welcome,' he said, smiling broadly, 'to our Aladdin's Cave.' And then he bowed theatrically and pushed open the door.

Sera gasped as she entered the long, surprisingly cool room, as an explosion of colour greeted her: jewel colours in bolts stacked high on shelves, more bolts lined up to attention on the floor like soldiers, all adorned with glittering gems in patterns reminiscent of starbursts or flowers or patterned swirls, sparkling where the light caught them. It was an endless array of colour—wherever she looked an endless source of delight.

Tucked into one corner of the vast room, a small display had been set up. Inadequate. really, given the extent of the range, but there was a bed, with covers and drapes and cushions, all aimed to show how the fabrics could be used. And alongside was set a trio of dummies, wearing gowns fashioned from the lightest fabric. The colours were intense, in ruby-red and sunset-gold and peacock-blue, the fabrics diaphanous, gossamer-thin, the emerald chips blazing upon them as if they were alive.

They were superb.

Rafiq was no less impressed. In truth, he'd expected a few bolts of fabric, some of it failing to live up to the sample his mother had shown him, because surely they would have sent their best to the Sheikha. But, looking at the vast selection around him, Rafiq wondered how anyone could have chosen the best.

He walked around the room, testing a sample of fabric here and there, admiring the handiwork, feeling the difference in the weights. He knew little of fabric, preferring to leave the finer details to his buyers' expertise, but he did know from the sales reports that anything of this quality would be snapped up in a heartbeat. Curtains, cushions, soft furnishings—even without the benefit of the mocked-up display, he could see the applications would be vast.

'Why is there so much here?' he wondered out loud, while Suleman stood rocking back on his heels, clearly delighted with his visitors' reactions.

'Abizah told us it was not the time to sell before now, and so we waited. The materials have been stockpiled here.'

Rafiq looked up. 'Abizah? The old woman we met?'

The elder nodded. 'Some said that she knew nothing of what she spoke, but others, mostly the women, overruled them.'

'Then how is it that I saw a bolt of this fabric at the palace just yesterday?'

'Ah.' Their guide nodded. 'There was one bolt, sent to the palace as a gift in the hope that it would be found suitable for a role in the coronation. Alas, we sent the fabric too late. The ceremonial robes had already been decided upon.'

Rafiq considered his words, accepted the sense they made. 'And your Abizah believes now is the right time to sell?'

'The moon is past full this month, and so, yes, she has given her approval. The time is upon us, she said.'

'My mother mentioned you already have somebody interested in the collection. How did they find out about what you have here?'

Suleman shrugged, holding his hands up, tilting his head, his brown face collapsing into craggy ravines as he smiled. 'Chance. Destiny. Who can say? A tourist couple, a businessman and his wife, they chanced across Marrash and stopped for refreshment. The women invited the wife in to view their treasures. As fate would have it, her husband was an executive for a large import company. He sent out a representative as soon as he returned home.'

Rafiq nodded. The man would have to have been certifiable not to. 'And an offer has been made?'

Suleman's chest puffed up with pride. 'A very good offer. Some said we should accept it straight away, that good fortune had shone down on Marrash the day the travellers happened by.'

'And others?'

Again that shrug, less pronounced this time. 'Others said that we should wait, that we had already waited this long and that we need not rush at the first sheep through the pen.'

The old Qusani proverb brought a smile to Rafiq's lips. It was a long time since he'd heard it, but the saying was uncannily pertinent. Why get excited chasing the fastest beast when it could be leaner and less tasty, when the slower animal might have more meat, more fat, and be more succulent and tender?

Rafiq's business sense kicked in, his pulse quickening at the thrill of the chase. He'd been given this opportunity, this chance to find something truly unique, and, while running his business and overseeing the big picture had consumed his time in the last few years, there was something to be said for the nitty-gritty of finding the actual items that would sell.

His gut had made him rich when he had first started out, many years ago, before he'd had buyers scouring the Arab world for the best. His gut had told him what items would work in the Australian market. His gut was telling him now that this was a rare find.

He owed his mother thanks. If she had not thought to show him the bolt of fabric he could have been too late, the deal already done.

'Are you able to tell me what this representative offered?'

Suleman gave an average figure per bolt—hopelessly inadequate, Rafiq recognised right away, even if Suleman had, as he expected he would have, inflated that figure with a decent margin to ensure any counter-offer would be better. But even if inflated, the quality of the fabrics at stake, let alone the rights to exclusivity, demanded at least that much again. Clearly the people of Marrash were being taken advantage of.

'It is not nearly enough,' he announced. 'You should be demanding at least double that.'

Beside him Sera gasped, as if she'd mentally calculated the worth of the room at the mention of the first offer, only to find Rafiq willing to offer double that price. But it was Suleman who looked the most taken aback, his face pale with shock. 'Are you making an offer, Your Highness?'

'Would it be accepted, Suleman?'

He bowed, his features quickly schooled, though his eyes shone with an excitement that refused to be masked. 'I would have to refer your offer to the council.'

'Of elders?' If so, with Suleman's clear excitement, the dollar signs practically spinning in his eyes, he would be home and hosed.

'Not in this case, Your Highness. It would be the women's council. It may sound unconventional, but this project has been the domain of the women all along. In deference to your position, they asked me to be their representative today.'

'Unconventional indeed,' he said. Not to mention disappointing. But hopefully the council of women might be influenced by the most senior of the village elders, just the same.

'It stems back to how the project began,' the elder continued, sounding apologetic. 'One of the women in the village, an aging widow, inherited some money from a family member in Shafar. She could simply have moved back to the city, but she had been in the village a long time and wanted to stay. She did not need the money for herself, so she elected to do something that would benefit the village as a whole, creating an ongoing income stream for all the women.'

Rafiq's eyebrows lifted in appreciation. 'A remarkable thing to do,' he said, and Suleman nodded sagely.

'Indeed. Already the women had been experimenting with off-cuts from the emerald mines, using the chips in all kinds of endeavours—the necklace from Abizah, for example...' he gestured towards the choker at Sera's neck '...and the lamp. They devised a method of using the emerald chips, of fracturing off tiny shards that would work like beads upon the fabrics. The inheritance supported the purchase of sewing machines and fabrics—the satins and silks that are the base of the finished product like those you see around you.'

'And because it is the women's endeavour, they are the ones who get to select the buyer—is that right?'

Suleman nodded, somewhat apologetically. 'They will listen to the advice of the council of elders, but ultimately, yes, it is their decision.'

'Could I meet with them, do you think? I would like to commend them on their endeavours.'

'They would most certainly be honoured, Your Highness. They are all working in the workshop nearby. Although...' Suleman coughed into his hand, his face serious, as if deliberating over his words carefully.

'Is there a problem?'

Suleman wavered, the creases at his brow deepening as he took a thoughtful breath. 'It is indeed the decision of the Marrashi women to make—and they will, of course, be honoured to meet you and show you their workroom—but I must warn you, the women do not feel confident in negotiating with a man. *Any man.* I am sorry, but it would be best if you left the negotiations to your companion.' He nodded towards Sera.

It was as his mother had said. She had advised him he would need a woman to negotiate any deal with the villagers.

He looked over to where Sera stood meekly at his shoulder, her dark eyes wide with concern, as if terrified by the prospect of speaking to the women's council on his behalf. But he saw beyond that too, stirring once again at the near perfection of her features, the perfection he would find if only she would smile again.

Need curled around him like a viper and tugged tight. At her throat the necklace of emerald chips winked and glinted in the light like a living thing, perhaps given life by the beating pulse at her throat that continued to fascinate him.

And he was suddenly consumed with the need to touch her, to slide his body along hers, to attain completion inside her slender form.

Release.

That was what he needed. That was what he wanted.

Release, and that secret smile she used to give him that gave an even warmer glow than the sun.

He breathed deep, knowing that one would come this night, perhaps, and, if he were lucky, both.

He turned back to Suleman, if only to remind himself that he was still here, and so as not to take Sera right now where she stood.

'Sera is here,' he managed to growl through a throat thick with need, 'for just that purpose.'

The older man nodded. 'I am glad you understand. I should also warn you the women's council likes to deliberate over its decisions, and it is highly unlikely that you will have a decision today, despite your generous offer.'

'I am not in Qusay for long,' Rafiq stressed, trying to impress upon Suleman some kind of urgency. 'I must return to Australia after the coronation, and it would make sense to have any deal nutted out before then.'

The older man nodded. 'I understand. However, the council of women has waited this long. It will most likely not choose to be rushed.'

The slow lamb, Rafiq thought. They would want a rich and plump beast, with meat enough for all to share. He doubted the other party would match his offer, but there was a possibility they would want to go back to find out. And then what? How long would the council of women keep waiting in order to get the fatted lamb?

Damn. If he was permitted to be the one to negotiate, he had no doubt he'd be able to turn them around—even if it was an entire roomful of women he was facing. He had a wealth of experience at negotiating mammoth business decisions behind him. It was the stuff he dealt with every day.

But Sera? She had no experience with such matters. No background in negotiating that he knew of.

Most important of all, she had no stake in the outcome. Apart from putting his offer to them, why should she argue for anything more—especially now she'd heard the women would probably want to take their time? Why should she rock the boat? It was no skin off her nose if he missed out on the deal.

Besides, how did he know she wouldn't deliberately sabotage him as payback for being forced to come out here with him?

But there was nothing he could do. So instead he growled out his understanding, already feeling the buzz of discovery waning with the possibility that the deal he'd felt so close to making might yet slip away.

Most likely would, now that it was in Sera's hands.

CHAPTER EIGHT

'How did you do it?' They'd not been long settled, or as settled as one could be, in the car that now rattled and lurched its way away from Marrash and down the mountainside, the sun slipping to the west on one side, its slanted rays colouring the cliffs an even more vibrant red. In the front seat one driver was offering the other his unappreciated advice from the passenger seat as to which set of ruts to follow, while Rafiq stared disbelievingly down at the paper in his lap—the paper Sera had provided him with after her meeting, and the paper that guaranteed him exclusive rights to the Marrash Collection, as the women's council had decided to call it.

Of course the lawyers would have to convert the hastily written scrawl into something resembling a legal document, with all the 'i's dotted and 't's crossed, and there would be signatures and counter-signatures required before it was all done and dusted, but the guts of it was done, the basic contract terms agreed.

But he still didn't understand how. Three hours or so ago they'd entered the sweetly perfumed building that housed the women's workshop to the whir and hum of a dozen sewing machines and the sound of the chatter and laughter of a score of women. Through it all had come the melodic tones of a lullaby, as a young woman soothed a baby in a corner of the room set up as a crèche. All had fallen silent at the arrival of the visitors, even the baby stopping its fussing as the room descended into an unexpected hush.

It hadn't lasted. The women, initially shy but more than delighted to accept their prince's compliments on their endeavours, had proudly showed him and Sera around their workshop, and then into the adjoining room, where another small group of women polished the tiny flakes of precious stone and transformed them into the shimmering beauties that would adorn fabrics or other souvenirs.

After the tour the women had apologised and begged Rafiq and Suleman to leave them with Sera while they deliberated. Suleman had done his best to distract the prince with a further walk through the village, relaying its long and ancient history and introducing citizens of interest along the way, but Rafiq had found it impossible to focus. Even knowing that there was little chance of any kind of agreement today, just knowing Sera was negotiating in his place was akin to having an iron chain knotted tight around his gut. What was the point of leaving someone else negotiating in his place? Especially when that woman was Sera.

It did not bode well.

'How long will they take?' Rafiq had asked, when they'd been an hour already, when already the wait had seemed interminable, but Suleman had merely smiled and shrugged his shoulders sympathetically.

'We are talking about a council of women,' he had replied, and Rafiq had taken his point even while the knotted chain around his gut had drawn tighter.

What was happening in there?

Until finally the women had emerged, smiling, from their meeting, and to his surprise Sera had presented him with the paper and the done deal. In relief, nothing more than relief, he'd picked her up and spun her in his arms and kissed her, to the cheers and whoops of everyone around.

But there had been no time to talk to her then, no time to check the details or to question how it had come about, for suddenly it had seemed the entire village had come out to celebrate the good news. And if he had thought the coffee pot had been constantly refreshed before, this afternoon it hadn't just been bottomless, it had been damn near eternal. Even if he'd wanted to get back to Shafar tonight, to make Kareef's state banquet, it would have been nigh on impossible to leave the celebrations in time.

Which gave him the perfect excuse. Now there was no choice but to stop at the coastal encampment a second night.

Amazing that fate had played into his hands so conveniently. Now his task would be so much easier. Sera could not be surprised when he made his move. Now they had something to celebrate. *Together.*

But still he didn't understand how this twist of fate had come about.

'How did you make it happen?' he asked again of the woman sitting alongside him in the back seat. Sera looked composed and serene, as always, but if he wasn't mistaken another layer of that cloak of sadness was gone, he was sure, and the corners of her mouth were turned up just the slightest fraction, as if she were just the tiniest bit pleased with herself as she contemplated his question.

She gave a tiny shrug. 'I liked meeting them. Strong women, determined to make a difference in their lives, working hard to achieve it.'

They had to be, Rafiq decided, for them to be doing what they were doing. But that still didn't answer the question that was uppermost in his mind. 'But Suleman said the women's council would most likely take its time. How did you manage to get their agreement to go to contract today?'

And Sera almost smiled, the merest shadow of a smile, and it was more than just the sloping rays of the sun's setting light playing upon her perfect features.

'You made it easier, to start with, for the women were almost beside themselves with your offer,' she told him. 'The previous offer had seemed a dream come true for all of them, a validation of everything they had hoped for, but your offer to double it was like a gift from the gods. They would be doubly blessed, and Abizah's pleas to wait seemed to have been vindicated.

'Yet still,' she continued softly, 'some thought that perhaps they should seek a counter-offer from the other party, to see if they could increase the offer even more.'

He nodded. *The fatted lamb*. Hadn't Suleman warned him of just such a likelihood? 'But they decided not to go that route. What happened to change their minds?'

'It was a close decision. The first vote was tied, and for a while all seemed to be at a stalemate. I guess they might have been waiting for me to offer more money, I don't know, but I felt that was not my place as you had given me no such authority to do so. So instead we left behind the thoughts of contracts and we just talked, as women do, about the recent developments in the royal family: of Xavian's—*Zahir's*—unexpected abdication, and about Prince Kareef and the upcoming coronation.'

Rafiq battled to find an answer to his questions in what she was saying. If there was one to be found, it eluded him. But he did find satisfaction, and a grudging degree of respect, in the fact she hadn't tried to increase his offer. It would have been easy enough for her to do so. After all, it wasn't her money she'd be spending, and she knew how much he wanted the deal wrapped up. 'And then what happened?'

And this time she did smile. Her hands crossed in her lap, and her eyes slanted ever so slightly towards him, as if sharing a secret joke. She was wearing an enigmatic smile that would have made the Mona Lisa proud. 'I was thinking about that bolt of fabric sent to the palace and of what that meant to the people of Marrash.'

He scrambled to make sense of the connection. 'And?'

Her smile broadened. 'Because it's one thing—a wonderful thing!—to be able to sell your goods to businesses that can afford them, wherever they are based in the world, but it seemed to me that there was a lingering disappointment in that room. Nothing would have been more important for the women of Marrash, nothing more satisfying while the eyes of the world were upon Qusay, than their fabrics being showcased during the coronation ceremony itself.'

'But it's too late to change that!' Rafiq growled, raking one hand through his hair in frustration, turning his face to the window in disappointment mingled with disgust. The ceremony was just a few short days away. If Sera had offered the Marrashi fabrics a place in the coronation the contract would be unstuck before it could even be drawn up by the lawyers and he would be back where he started. Worse. He would have a disappointed and no doubt uncooperative business partner into the deal. 'You can't expect them to change the arrangements for the coronation at this short notice.'

'I don't!' she came back, her reaction so vehement after all her meekness of before that he was suddenly reminded in one instant of how she once had been, years ago. Vibrant, and filled with life and laughter. And he swung his head back, the offence she'd taken at his words so plain on her features that he felt it like a slap to his own face.

She sat up, impossibly stiff and rigid against her seat, the smile he'd waited for and celebrated when it had finally arrived now vanquished. 'It just seemed, from what was said while the women talked, that the women would really value their work being recognised and admired in their own country. They knew the collection would be sold to the highest bidder, and that made good economic sense to them, but they also needed to have their work showcased and celebrated by their own. The coronation seemed to them the perfect time that this might happen, while the eyes of the world were upon them. But, as you say, it is too late for that to happen now.'

'So what did you suggest?'

She bit down on her lip, and looked out of her window for a second before swinging her head back. 'I merely suggested that if—*if*—they accepted your offer, that one day, when you married, with the eyes of the world upon a royal wedding, you might wish your bride to wear a gown fashioned from the most glorious fabrics that the Marrashi women could provide.'

He blinked, slow and hard. 'You promised *what*? A royal marriage? A wedding gown? But I have no plans for marriage—*ever*! Which means no bride for the women of Marrash to dress. What kind of position do you think that puts me in? What the hell were you thinking?'

She snapped her head around, her dark eyes flaring like coals. 'I was thinking you wanted the deal closed today!'

'But to promise them a wedding. *My* wedding!'

'I could hardly promise them Prince Kareef's! He will no doubt have to marry soon, to provide the kingdom with an heir, but I could hardly commit him to the same arrangement when the deal is purely to benefit you!'

She dragged in a breath as she cast her eyes downwards, and when she resumed her voice was softer, more controlled, reminding him of how she had sounded, so meek and docile, when they had started this journey. He hated how it sounded.

'I did not say that a marriage would definitely take place, or when, but I thought you, at least, would understand my reasoning. It is important to the women that their fabrics and their expertise be recognised in their own land. And what else did you give me to negotiate with?'

'I never gave you a wedding!' But even as he said the words he realised how churlish he sounded. He growled in irritation and turned his head away, knowing the cliff at his side had more cracks and faults than her logic. She'd got the women's agreement. She'd got the contract in the space of one not entirely short meeting.

And yet marriage…?

Sera had built into the negotiations an expectation from the women of the village that he would marry. The women would expect it now. The women would be waiting for any hint…

And his mind reeled back to the cheers and whoops that had met his impulsive reaction when Sera had emerged with the news.

He had kissed her.

Sera.

And the women had cheered and laughed and cried their blessings. Their laughter had made him remember he wasn't in Australia, that it wasn't the usual thing to pick up any unmarried woman, even if a widow, and kiss her in public.

But still he'd thought they were merely celebrating the contract.

But they wouldn't be delighted, would they? They'd normally be shocked at such bold behaviour.

Unless…

And suddenly the chains that had worked their way so tightly around his gut this day started tightening their grip around his neck. The women of Marrash expected that Sera would be his bride. Hadn't Abizah already assumed that she was?

He turned to her. 'The women think I'm going to marry you. It is *our* wedding they are contemplating. It is you they see wearing the bridal gown of Marrash.'

She was shaking her head, her eyes swirling with panic.

Because she'd been caught out? 'No, I'm sure they don't think that.'

'I kissed you.'

Still her head shook from side to side. Her cheeks flushed, as if the very idea was anathema to her too, and that only made him more annoyed. *She should be so lucky!*

'You didn't mean anything by it. You didn't know. You weren't to know. It meant nothing.'

And even he, who wanted it to mean nothing, who needed it to have meant nothing, had to question her words. *Had* it meant nothing? Then why had it felt as if he had poured everything into that kiss? His frustrations at waiting, at not being permitted to negotiate himself. His relief when Sera had emerged victorious from the meeting. All of it he had poured into one impulsive kiss as he had spun her around, the feel and taste of her lush lips giving him a thirst for more, a thirst he intended to slake tonight.

So maybe that kiss *had* meant something—a physical need, an itch that had never been scratched. But it still didn't mean...

He leaned across the seat and put his arm around her shoulders, drawing her close, murmuring in her ear so that those in the front seat could not hear, so close that in other circumstances his words might almost be interpreted as a lover's caress. He touched the fingers of his other hand to her cheek, drinking in the softness with the pads of his fingers until she shuddered under his touch.

'I won't marry you, Sera. It doesn't matter what the women of Marrash think. It doesn't matter what anyone thinks. I won't marry you. *Ever.* Because there is no way I could marry you after what you did.'

There was a pause. A slowing of the earth's rotation while he heard her hitched intake of air, while he waited for her eyelids to open after they'd been jammed so firmly shut.

before finally she acknowledged his words with a slow nod, her smile once again reappearing in a way that rubbed raw against him.

'Don't you think I know that?' Her voice was hushed but the tone was rapier-sharp. 'Don't you think I've lived with the knowledge that you must surely hate me for what happened all those years ago? I realise that. I understand it. And what makes you imagine for a moment that I need another man in my life? What makes you think I need or want *you*? I came up with the idea of the wedding gown for your bride so that you might win the deal. Not because I was somehow trying to engineer a wedding between the two of us.'

And his barb of irritation grew sharper and more pointed, working its way deeper into his flesh. She was a widow and he was now a prince—a wealthy prince. He could give her everything she wanted: status, money and privilege. And now she was saying she didn't want him.

She did. Of that he was sure.

So he didn't let her go. Instead, he toyed with her hair with a playfulness he didn't feel, weaving his fingers through its heavy silken curtain, trying hard not to pull it tight, trying hard not to pull her face against his. 'That's not how it looked to the Marrashis.'

She kicked up her chin, glared at him, resentment firing her eyes. 'And whose fault is that?'

His fingers curled and flexed with aggravation before they would relax enough for him to be able to stroke her neck, and he felt the tremor under her skin even as she tried to suppress it. 'I'm not the one who put the wedding idea into their heads.'

'And I'm not the one who kissed you!'

His eyes dropped to her lips, slightly parted. Her breathing was fast, her chest rising and falling with the motion.

Maybe not, he thought, but she hadn't been an unwilling

party. He remembered the feel of her mouth under his own, her delight at her success right there to be tasted on her lips, and the way she had so easily melted into his kiss. Neither would she be an unwilling party now—he'd bet on it.

All it would take would be to curl that hand around her neck and draw her closer.

He breathed deep, looking for strength but instead filling himself with her beguiling scent, the herbs that she used to rinse her black hair, the soap she used against her satin skin.

Twice now he'd kissed her—impulsive, unplanned kisses that had ended abruptly, leading nowhere but to frustration— kisses that had been doomed to come to nothing from the very beginning because they had not been alone.

But still those kisses had given him something. Two things. A taste for more, and the knowledge that she wanted him. She might say she didn't want to marry him, but she wanted him. He'd as good as read her confession in the tremors that plagued her skin when he touched her—he'd read it in the way her mouth opened under his. Her melting bones had told him. She wanted him. Of that he was sure.

And right now that was the only truth that mattered.

He smiled at her, finally tearing his eyes from her lips to see her looking uncertain, bewildered, almost as if she had expected he was going to kiss her again, almost as if she had anticipated the press of his lips against hers.

And his smile widened.

'Don't be disappointed,' he whispered, so close to her ear that he could feel the soft down of her earlobe, his lips tickled by the cool gold of the hoop that circled through it. 'I will kiss you again. But not now. Not yet. For the next time I kiss you it will be somewhere we cannot be interrupted.'

And this time she trembled in his embrace, her dark eyes conveying surprise. More than surprise, he noticed. For there was the smoke of desire there too, turning them cloudy and filled with need.

He breathed deep, dragging in more of the air flavoured with her signature scent, letting it feed his senses. For now, in the back seat of a car, descending a mountain track, it would have to be enough.

He squeezed her shoulder one last time before sliding his arm out from behind her, stretching back into his own seat, for the first time noticing the sunset that blazed red and gold in the distance as the vehicle wound its way down the switchback road. Soon it would be night, and they would stay once more at the encampment by the sea. Which meant that soon he would have her.

He took another desperate gulp of air, suddenly needing the oxygen, needing to shift in his seat to accommodate his growing tightness. Maybe he should concentrate on the sunset for now, instead of what might come after. But knowing that made no difference. For it was near impossible to drag his mind away from thoughts of Sera in his arms, her long limbs naked and wound around him as he plunged into her silken depths.

How long had he dreamed about this night? How long had those visions plagued him? Tonight, though, the dreams would become reality. Tonight she would be his.

He growled on an exhale, trying to dispel some of his burgeoning need. Admiring the sunset would be safer. For it was a stunning sunset: the sun a fireball sinking lower, the sky awash with colour.

Colour.

Which reminded him of the package he'd brought with him—the only purchase Suleman had permitted him to negotiate himself. He reached behind the seat for it, but stopped when he saw Sera huddled alongside, pressed tight against the door, her eyes lost, her expression bleak as her hands twisted first at her necklace and then in her lap.

And something shifted in his gut: guilt, emerging in an unfamiliar bubble. What had caused her sudden misery when so recently she had been warm for him? Had he provoked this slide into desolation?

He almost reached out to her. Almost lifted a hand to touch her. To reassure her.

But just as quickly he snatched his hand back, snuffing out the notion. Because that would mean he cared. And he didn't care. Not really. He wanted her—there was no doubting that. But caring? He had long since given up caring about Sera.

Besides, he thought, shrugging off the unfamiliar sense of guilt, what evidence did he have that he had upset her? For all he knew she could be thinking about Hussein and wishing he were still here.

He swung his head away, disgusted with himself. That thought was no consolation. Hussein might have been her husband for a decade, but he did not want her so much as thinking about the man.

Not that it would last. Tonight he would drive every memory of Hussein from her thoughts.

Tonight she would discover what she had missed.

CHAPTER NINE

IT WAS impossible. Sera shrank further back into the leather of her seat, not understanding what had just transpired. There had been brief moments today when Rafiq had seemed different, when they had seemed to be able to share the same planet without sniping at each other. But they had gone from discussing the day's success to suddenly being at each other's throats—before the atmosphere had changed again and suddenly become more charged. More intense.

More dangerous.

She fingered the emerald choker at her neck as she stared out of her window, remembering the feel of Rafiq's fingers as he had secured it around her neck—more a lover's caress than that of a man who abhorred her. She despaired of the inconsistency, wishing she could focus on the glorious sunset instead of having these thoughts constantly thrashing through her mind. Wishing even more that she could control her own wayward emotions. But there was no focus. No control.

For every time he had looked at her today, every time he'd been near, she had felt the increasing pull between them, the flare of desire that charged the air with a shimmering need, a force that served to draw them together.

And when he touched her—the pad of his fingers against

her neck, the lacing of his fingers through her hair—it was simply electric.

Had anyone else around them felt it? Could anyone else tell?

She sighed against the glass. Of course they could. They all could. The women had seen him kiss her. Everyone had seen the way she'd spun in his arms as if she belonged there.

Everyone knew—even, it seemed, a woman whose cataracts had nearly blinded her. And was it any wonder, when she felt her own need so badly?

For how had she reacted when he had told her he would kiss her again? Not with outrage or anger, or even offence at his arrogant statement. No! Instead she'd looked at him with big puppy eyes, sad because she'd missed out on the treat of him kissing her then, suddenly excited because he'd given her the promise of a kiss later, *when there was no chance they would be interrupted.*

Tremors ran down her spine anew, shooting out laterally through soft tissue to find nerve-endings too receptive, too ready to surge into life. She squeezed her eyes shut, dragged in air, trying unsuccessfully to deny the sensory assault. Why did his promise fill her with such fear and such anticipation at the same time? Why was she so suddenly conscious of her swelling breasts, her nipples, and the insistent yearning between her thighs? How could he reduce her to this when she felt so ashamed?

She had to stop herself from crying out with the unfairness of it all. Why should she feel so much, so intensely? She was no teenager any more. She was a mature woman. Perhaps not as experienced as most, but she'd been a wife, a married woman, for almost a decade. She'd long since buried her teenage hopes and wishes, just as she'd buried her body's needs and desires under a public face that aimed for serenity. Control. Cool composure.

Why, now, should her body betray her?

For ten years she had felt nothing, suppressed all her desires and wishes and needs until she was sure they were banished for ever. And now, instead of serene and cool and calm, she felt hot and agitated, her skin tingling in places she'd thought long since devoid of feeling, as if all the emotions and unrecognised desires of the past ten years were welling up to engulf her in one tidal wave of emotion.

She was like that teenager all over again—the girl who had fallen head over heels in love with a tall, golden-skinned Qusani, with piercing blue eyes and a magnetism that had bound her to him from the first instant they'd met.

Even then she'd felt this way around him—this heightened sense of awareness, as if he was caressing her without even touching her. But why, more than ten years on, should he still affect her this way? It wasn't as if she was still in love with him.

And she gasped, a new realisation slamming through her like a thunderbolt.

She couldn't be!

Surely there was no way?

She squeezed her eyes shut, prayed she was mistaken. She was taken aback, that was all—taken aback at his sudden re-appearance. Thrown off-balance at their forced proximity these last few hours.

It could be nothing more than that, surely?

For once before she had lost him; once before she had seen him go. And once before it had all but ripped her heart from her chest.

Soon he would return to his business in Australia and she would watch him leave once again.

No, she could not love him. She dared not.

Oh, no, please not that!

But there came no denials, no safety ramp to save her as the brakes failed on her reason. Instead came only the constant thrum beat of her heart, pounding out what she had denied for so many years, what she had hoped to suppress for ever.

She loved him.

The rest of the journey down the mountainside passed in a blur, a jumble of confused emotions and tangled thoughts. None of them helping. None of them sorting out the morass that had become her mind. But at least Rafiq left her to her despair. She could not have handled conversation when her mind was in such turmoil, her thoughts in such disarray, disbelief the only continuous thread. They'd stopped at the campsite before she'd even realised.

It was Rafiq who opened her door, his blue eyes moving to a frown as he took in her startled face. 'What's wrong?' he growled.

She blinked and took a deep breath of the warm sea air, un-latching her seat belt, realising that even by merely drifting off she had annoyed him. Although maybe sleep was what she needed? Maybe it would make some sense out of the tangle of her thoughts.

And then she put her hand in his to climb down, and felt the charge like a shockwave up her arm. She gasped, and his eyes snagged hers, and the hungry gleam in his eyes told her that he'd felt it too.

So much for making sense.

She moved away as soon as she could, putting distance between them, confused when she saw the drivers already un-loading things from the back of the car. Other servants who had stayed at the camp today were coming to assist, making long shadows against the tents in the light of the torches. She was further confused when she detected the aroma of lamb mixed with herbs on the breeze.

'How long are we stopping?' she asked, as she stood on a dune overlooking the long, pristine beach, under a sky embla zoned with stars. But they did not hold her attention—not when she became more concerned as more and more was unloaded from the car.

'Until morning. We are camping here again overnight.'

She turned, surprised to find that he was so close, surprised even more by his answer. She'd hoped they'd be back in the palace tonight. She'd hoped she'd be once again tucked away in her room in the Sheikha's apartments, where she could lie in her bed and try to forget about Rafiq all over again. But another night out here with him, after what he'd told her...

Would he kiss her tonight? Here in the camp? Was that his intention, before she could be tucked safely away in his mother's quarters at the palace?

She swallowed. She remembered last night, when he'd hijacked her peaceful swim at the end of the beach and refused to give her back her *abaya*. She remembered the way his eyes had seared a trail over her skin—how it had made her breasts come alive, her senses buzz and quicken with expectation. No way would she risk that tonight! For tonight she wouldn't trust herself to coolly walk away.

'I thought you wished to return to Shafar as soon as possible once the deal was done.'

'It is not safe to drive through the desert at night with only one vehicle.' He raised an eyebrow, the flickering torches turning his golden skin to red, making him look more dangerous than ever. 'Some might say it is not safe even to drive through the desert during the day.'

Heat flooded her cheeks at the reference. Was it only one day ago that she'd driven the other car into the sinking sands? So much seemed to have happened since then. So little time, but enough to throw her entire world upside down.

'But is there not a state banquet at the palace tonight? We could press on, return to the palace as soon as possible, surely?'

He shrugged, unmoved by her need to return to Shafar. 'It is too late to get there, even if we left now. Besides, it will not be the first or the last time that I miss a state banquet. After all, I am merely—what did you call me?—a tourist prince…'

This time she gasped, her hands flying to her mouth. 'Rafiq, I was so wrong. I saw you with the people of Marrash. I saw how you related to them and how they took to you. I should never have said such a thing. I had no right.'

He hushed her words by holding two fingers to her lips, enjoying the way they parted underneath his fingers, as if she were shocked by his touch. 'No. You had no right. But you did make me think. Last night at the beach, for the first time you made me think about what kind of prince I could be. I have not lived here for many years. I know nothing of politics, or the things that matter to the people. But I have not got to where I am now without knowing that I will succeed at anything I turn my hand to. I will be a good prince of Qusay, Sera, a strong prince.'

She swallowed. 'I can see that.'

'And I will start now, with my first royal command. You will dine with me tonight, in my tent.'

His voice was gruff and low, his command scraping against her senses, and his eyes, his blue eyes, were heavy with want. The combination sent vibrations deep down inside her. 'Is… Is that wise?'

And he smiled—a lean, hungry smile. 'It is what I command. That is all you need to know.'

She dropped her eyes to the ground. 'Of course.'

'And Sera?' He retrieved a package from the back seat of the car and returned to where she stood, almost invisible in her dark gown, knowing if just for that reason that he was right about this.

'What is it?'

'Open it and see for yourself. Suleman would not let me ne gotiate on anything but this.'

She slipped the tie binding the package slowly off its ends, unwrapped the paper, and gasped as a burst of blue, bright and sparkling in the flare of the torchlight, met her eyes. For a second she thought it was merely fabric, and then she recognised it.

'The dress,' she cried, recognising one of the gowns she'd seen on the models in the small corner display. She lifted it by one shoulder, admiring how the stones winked at her in the light from the torches, before noticing the flash of red below it. The weight of the package told her there was more. She dug deeper and caught a hint of sunset-gold. 'You bought all three?'

'I wanted all three.'

'They're so beautiful.' Suddenly she frowned. 'But will such garments sell well in your country?'

He shook his head. 'These garments are not destined for my stores.'

The smooth skin between her eyes creased a fraction more. 'For the Sheikha, then?'

'I'm sure she would love them, but no.'

'Then why?'

'They are a gift. For you.'

And once again he had taken her unawares; once again he had sent her spirits into confusion.

She pressed the package back, the silken fabric heavy with gems sliding downwards. 'Rafiq, I cannot accept such a glorious gift.'

He pressed the package to her, scooping up the ends and bundling them into her hands. 'You can, and you will. For too long now you have buried your beauty under the colour of mourning. I knew it the moment I saw the emerald-green choker at your neck. It is time for you to reveal your beauty once more.'

His words hit a nerve she'd thought long buried. He knew that? She'd worn black initially out of the respect she must show for her dead husband, but then it had come to suit her, reflecting the dark hole her life had been, the dark hole her life had become. It had become a dark hole too deep, too convenient, to climb out of.

'But Rafiq…' She tried to hand the package back. She couldn't accept anything from him. No gift. Nothing.

'Take them, I command you.'

Her head tilted, the heavy curtain of black hair sliding over her shoulder with it, so sleek and shiny that he was tempted to run his hand through its weight, to feel the slide of its silken length through his fingers.

She had no choice but to accept the package. What was the point of objecting? How could she object? He was a prince.

But *colour*. She stroked the fabrics, drinking in their feel with her fingertips. For so long her life had been black and white, her feelings neutral to numb the pain. But now her senses had been reawakened, along with a yearning for the things she'd missed. Colour was one of them.

'Tonight you will wear the blue gown.'

She looked up at him, uncertain, her dark eyes wide. The stars in the night sky were reflected in their depths, he noticed, a galaxy of stars that along with the flicker of torchlight gave her eyes a molten glow. Soon, he knew, it would be him who turned them molten.

Later, in her tent, bathed but still shaking and breathless from the unexpected encounter, Sera held the blue gown up in front of her. What would it be like to wear such a bold colour? As much as she was tempted, after so many months of covering herself in black the idea of colour seemed somehow daring. Provocative.

Or was it just because of the way Rafiq had looked at her, with hunger in his eyes and a wicked smile curving his lips?

She dragged in air, needing the burst of oxygen. How could she decide when she could not so much as think rationally?

So, instead of thinking, she shrugged the gown over her shoulders, letting the weight of the stone-encrusted fabric pull it down over her skin. She felt the whisper of silk, the weight of tiny stones, and the close-fitting gown moved against her like the slide of a thousand fingers. And then it was on, and she looked once more in the small mirror and she saw someone else—a stranger, a woman she hadn't seen for more than a decade—standing before her. A few years older, maybe, but not so markedly different that she couldn't recognise the girl who had come before.

For a minute or two she just stared, before realising that it wasn't just the colour of her dress that made her look so different and turned back the clock. It was her eyes that had changed also. They looked alive, somehow. Excited. As they had so many years before. As they had when they'd been filled with love—and desire—for Rafiq.

The desire was still there.

Her heart fluttered in her chest and she gasped, unused for so long to feeling the heat of need, surprised by its power. She'd once put this feeling down to adolescence and the stirrings of the first tender buds of first love.

But it wasn't that now.

She'd tried to deny it because it was beyond modesty to think of such things—forbidden territory for a woman in her position to feel such raw, potent need.

She'd tried to deny it because she was so ashamed of her past. So ashamed of the things her body had been used for.

But there was no denying it.

She did want him. She did need him. And it didn't matter what happened after this—for destiny seemed determined to ʾeep them apart—it didn't matter that she'd married another when she'd loved Rafiq, it didn't matter that he'd sworn he'd never marry her now. There was no denying it. She wanted him.

Star-crossed they might be, destined never to be together, but maybe tonight, *this night*, they would become lovers.

She brushed her hair, giddy with anticipation, her blood fizzing in her veins at the recklessness of her thoughts. She'd never known the pleasure a man could give. She'd never known the magic she'd heard newly married women giggle about in muffled whispers to each other in the hallways of the palace. She'd never known the delights of the flesh.

Rafiq, she was sure, could supply them.

And why shouldn't she take advantage of this beachside encampment, just as Rafiq intended? Why should she not use it for her own purposes, to assuage her own desperate longings and desires?

Just one night, with a man who would never love her, never marry her. It was wrong on so many levels. And yet on so many more it was right.

She smoothed down her dress, garnering her resolve in the process. If he did intend to kiss her again tonight, if he did want them to be uninterrupted, she would not be the one to interrupt.

This night was like a gift from the gods. People said you didn't get a second chance, that you couldn't go back, and maybe they were right. Maybe there *was* no going back to the days when she had believed she and Rafiq would one day marry and share their lives together for ever. Those days were surely gone.

But one night—this night—was something. A glimpse, perhaps, of what might have been. A bittersweet reminder of what she had lost.

And something to hold close to her when he had gone from her life again. For he would leave soon, return to his business in Australia, forget about her all over again.

She would have this one night to remember for ever. She took one last, steeling breath of air, recognising the effort was futile, that she would never settle the butterflies that even now jostled for air space in her stomach, before she stepped from the tent.

All was prepared. Rafiq waited patiently. The table under the stars was prepared; the food was ready to serve. All that was needed was Sera.

Away from the tents he could hear the men talking around their campfire, the burble and fragrant scent of the *shisha* pipe carrying on the night breeze. A perfect evening, neither too hot nor too cool, with the blanket of stars a slow-moving picture overhead.

And then Sera appeared, and the night became even more perfect.

Shyly she approached the table, her eyes cast downwards. *Like a virgin*, he thought. A shy and timid innocent, on her way to be sacrificed. But she was no virgin, he knew. And it was not white that she wore. Nor even black, he acknowledged with relief. The blue gown skimmed her curves, fitting without catching anywhere, the shimmering gem-encrusted silk bringing her body alive in light and shadow as she moved, the jewels around her neck turning her into a glittering prize.

His prize.

'You look beautiful,' he said, his voice thicker than usual, and for the first time her eyes lifted, only to widen with shock when she saw him. 'Rafiq!'

And he smiled. 'A fair trade, wouldn't you say? My robe for your gown.'

'Rafiq, you look— You look…' *Devastating.* Her eyes drank him in—this man who wore Armani and turned it into an art form, this man who lifted a mere suit and made it an extension of his lean, powerful self, who looked like a god in the robes of his countrymen. The snowy-white robe turned his live skin to burnished gold, turned his black hair obsidian.

And his eyes—what it did to his eyes! They were like sapphires warmed by the light of the moon. Penetrating. Captivating.

He looked taller somehow, and even more commanding, and she had no doubt he was indeed a true prince of Qusay!

Finally she managed to untangle her useless tongue. 'I mean, you look different—almost like you belong here.'

And he laughed as she hadn't heard him laugh for so long, the sound rich and strong, his face turned up to the heavens and showing off the strong line of his throat. 'My mother will be delighted to hear it. She has been on at me to wear the traditional robes from the moment I arrived. But now come. Sit. Eat. For we are far from the palace, and tonight...' he swept his arm around in an arc '...this is our palace.'

His eyes seemed to glitter more brightly than any jewels she was wearing, his teeth shining white in his smile.

Staff appeared from nowhere, ready to serve and fill glasses and dishes, to perform every wish of their master, before fading back into the darkness of the night as the sea provided music, its endless swoosh and suck of the waves curling over the shore. Here, this night, she could believe he had embraced his role as prince. Here she could see the man had become more than a prince in name only.

'Doesn't it frighten you?' she asked softly, when the staff had edged back into the night. 'Knowing your brother will be king? To know that you are but one step from becoming king yourself?'

His face tightened. 'Nothing will happen to Kareef. Before long he will marry and have the heirs he needs and I will no longer be second in line to the throne. Besides which,' he said, attempting a smile, 'there is always Tahir.'

'Your younger brother? But nobody even knows where he is.'

Rafiq shook his head, not for the first time wondering where his wayward brother had got to. Maybe there would be som news when they returned to the palace. He shrugged. 'It is all academic. Kareef will make a fine King.'

A servant bowed and approached the pair then, asking if they needed anything more. Rafiq waved the intrusion away. Neither of them seemed to be hungry, merely picking at their food despite the tender herbed meat and freshly spiced vegetables. Instead they seemed content to drink each other in with their eyes, as if that was all the sustenance they needed.

It was all Rafiq needed. To see her like this, her beauty emblazoned in colour, for once highlighting instead of dragging down her dark beauty, was enough to sustain him.

Almost enough.

'Why did you do it?' he asked softly, when it was clear both of them were finished with eating, even though their plates were still full.

'Why did I do what?'

'Why did you bother to make a deal with the women's council? You could have accepted their position when they said they'd like to seek a counter-offer. You could have walked away then, knowing that Suleman had predicted such an outcome, knowing I'd half expected it. You could have walked away from the negotiation. After all, why should you care whether or not I got the deal? The way I've spoken to you, dragged you halfway across the desert against your wishes, why wouldn't you want to sabotage my chances?'

She leaned back in her chair, her eyes thoughtful, though it was the way the fabric tugged across her breasts that captured his gaze, and he felt his hunger building—though not for food.

She paused before answering, as if measuring her words, wanting to make each one count. 'I know it's hard for you to believe, Rafiq, but I was hoping to make up a little for the pain I caused you in the past. I am truly sorry for what happened, 'nd for the way you found out about my wedding.'

He growled, cursing himself for bothering to make conversation when all he wanted was to bury himself in her body. He wasn't interested in hearing her lame excuses again. 'You didn't look sorry at the time! You didn't sound sorry.'

'I don't… I can't expect you to believe me.'

'And how *can* I believe you? You keep saying you had no choice.'

If she'd looked away he might have felt differently. If she'd looked away he might have thought she'd had something to hide. But she held his gaze from under lids slumberous with intent, her eyes fixed level upon his. 'I had a choice,' she started, and he flinched and wished she had said something different. 'A choice that was made plain to me. I could protect my family's honour, with the promise of a plush job for my father, or he would ruin them for ever.'

'*He* would ruin them? Who do you mean?'

'Who do you think? Was he not there, gloating at the wedding, knowing it had all gone even more perfectly than he'd imagined?'

'What are you talking about?'

'Your father, Rafiq. Your own father threatened me, told me that a match between you and me would come to nothing. I already knew how badly Kareef had suffered, but when your father visited me, told me that he had plans for you, plans that included better than me, and that my entire family would suffer if I did not marry Hussein, what choice did I have? Do you really think I could have married Hussein otherwise? Do you really believe that?'

But Rafiq was still reeling from the discovery his father had had a hand in his betrayal. That it was his father who had been the one to force them apart. His own father.

Ever since their argument at the oasis yesterday it had bothered him. Sera had said then that she'd had no choice, th she couldn't bring the shame of Jasmine's family on her own, and in the white-hot heat of his fury he had refused to listen, refused to see her point of view.

But he had lived in Australia a long time. He had forgotten what life was like here—had failed to remember the expectations a father had for his daughters, had disregarded what it must have been like to live with the ever-present risk of shaming one's family by one's actions.

And he had never for a moment considered a father's expectations for his sons. His father had wanted to control every aspect of his sons' upbringing, had made every decision, and he had been beyond furious when Kareef had been rescued in the desert with Jasmine.

Of course he had wanted to choose their wives. Of course he would have considered it his choice. He had wanted to control their lives. Instead, he had driven them all away, one by one.

It made some kind of sense. Even his own mother taking Sera in. No wonder she felt responsible. No wonder she wanted to make amends.

Rafiq dragged fingers through his hair, nails raking his scalp. He had been blinded by his own hurt. His own pain. Rendered himself incapable of seeing anything else.

And while his mind reeled with his own inadequacies, another snippet managed to filter through. His mind spun backwards, desperate to replay the words…

'…*when your father visited me, told me that he had plans for you, plans that included better than me, and that my entire family would suffer if I did not marry Hussein, what choice did I have? Do you really think I could have married Hussein otherwise?*'

A tidal wave could not have hit him with more force. 'You didn't want to marry him. You didn't love him.'

And this time she did turn her head away, as if she couldn't bear to look at him while she spoke of her husband. 'I never loved him!'

There was a chill in her words that he didn't understand, couldn't compute, but there was no time to analyse that now, no time to think of anything but the incredible satisfaction of knowing she had never loved her husband. 'And when you told me, in front of everyone, that you had never loved me…'

She dropped her face into her hands. 'I lied.' Her voice was as thin as the golden thread that held the tiny gems to her gown, and he felt her words run ice-cold through his veins.

He thrust his hands once more through his hair, the pain of his nails raking his scalp nowhere near enough to wipe away the pain in his heart. He wanted to believe her. So much. But still it wasn't enough. Because it hadn't just been the words she'd spoken. It had been the evidence of his own eyes that had damned her, and still did.

'But it wasn't just what you told me, was it? I saw you at the reception! I saw him pull you to him. I saw him practically thrust his tongue down your throat, his hand mauling your breast. And I saw you reaching out your own hand to his lap, squeezing him like you'd never touched me! Everyone was busy watching the dancers, but I witnessed it all. And I wanted to tear him limb from limb. It was only Kareef who managed to talk sense into me, holding me back and telling me to go, to leave you, to get out while I still could.'

'And you would have seen me run out to be sick, but you had already gone!' Her voice was but a whisper, a thin thread that sounded as if at any moment it might snap. 'Hussein liked you watching. He revelled in the jealousy he saw in your expression.'

'Why did you do it? How could you do it?'

'He threatened me. Said if you kept coming after me he would hurt you. Not enough to enrage your father, but enough to teach you a lesson.' Her head sagged further towards her lap. 'I couldn't let that happen. I had to convince you that we were over. If you wouldn't believe my declaration that I'd never loved you, there was no other way but to do as he said.'

Mechanically he left his chair, crossed to her side, all without consciously thinking about what he was doing. He knelt at her side, took her wrists in his hands, and peeled her hands away. Moisture clung to her closed lashes; her lips were jammed together.

'You did that to protect me?'

Her eyelids parted on dark eyes filled with pain. 'I was afraid—too afraid of what might happen if I did otherwise. He scared me.' She shuddered where she sat, her teeth biting her bottom lip white, the involuntary action telling him more than any words could.

'It's okay,' he said, taking her by the shoulders, coaxing her to her feet. 'It's all right.'

But she was shaking her head. 'It's not okay. You were supposed to be away for a year. I thought you might forget about me in that time. I thought it might not be so bad. When you turned up unexpectedly at the ceremony I had to do something to make you hate me. Something to make you accept what had happened. And so I lied. I acted like I loved him, like I wanted to be with him. But I never did, I swear.'

Her liquid eyes looked too huge for her face, the misery they contained too much for any one person to have to bear. 'And so you did love me. All along.'

Slowly she nodded, her lips tightly clenched between her teeth, tears once more flooding her eyes.

And he wanted to roar with possession, howl at the moon. For she had always been his. He had known it. She had been his from the very first moment they had laid eyes on each other.

And tonight he would take what had been rightfully his— would take what he had been denied, so long ago.

CHAPTER TEN

HE TOUCHED two fingers to her lips, smoothing away their tightness, taking her chin in his hand and guiding it higher. She was afraid, he could tell, her dark eyes filled with trepidation, her breathing jerky.

And her fear was no doubt his fault too, because every time she had tried to explain, to make amends, he had been blinded to her words and had refuted her every argument. He was the reason she had fled into the desert. It had been his words that had put her very life at risk.

'I'm sorry,' he told her, and her fear turned to confusion as he slid both hands over her slim shoulders into her thick black hair. 'I would not listen to you yesterday when you tried to explain. I made no attempt to understand. And it was from me you felt you needed to escape. It was me who put you in danger. Is there any chance you might forgive me?'

Her eyes wavered with uncertainty, colour rising like a tide in her cheeks, and her lips parted, closed, parted again, as if she were searching for words. 'I might,' she managed tentatively, pausing for air. 'If you… Do you think there is any chance you might still want to…kiss me again?'

And his lips turned into a smile as his eyes were drawn to her mouth, to her lips, lush and ripe, just as his body was drawn to hers, as it had been every single moment since they'd passed each other outside his mother's suite. 'You know that I want you,' he whispered, his mouth hovering scant millimetres above hers.

This time when her eyes widened, their dark depths stirred with something other than fear. 'I know.'

'And you want me.'

A pause, a blink, and then came the halting response, 'It's…true.'

'Because, like I said before, the next time I kiss you I won't stop.'

A hitch in her breath, a flare of her nostrils. 'I know. I'm scared, Rafiq. I'm scared I can't do this.'

He had her in his arms before his blood had stopped its tidal surge through his veins, his lips on hers before the crashing had stopped in his ears.

And this time it was neither a kiss of anger, wrenched from her, nor a kiss of spontaneous relief, but a deliciously anticipated act that spoke of mutual need and mutual pleasure, a journey of rediscovery and shared desires and ten long years. His lips moved over hers in an unchoreographed dance that she somehow knew, matching him move for move. Fitting him perfectly. Suiting him perfectly. Hot breath and the sweet taste of Sera filled his senses and he could not get enough, could not think straight beyond wanting her. Except for knowing they could not stay here.

He growled, low in his throat, the vibrations rumbling into the kiss as he untangled his hands from her hair, battled to untangle himself from the kiss. Sera felt them through the hard wall of chest, rippling through her as he swept her into his arms. 'Come,' he said, 'tonight you need not be afraid.'

And, suddenly uncertain, she felt the first seeds of panic worm their way into her bliss. 'Rafiq, there is something—'

But he had no use for words. Not any more. Not when he

had seen they could be used to distort and corrupt and crucify with such devastating effect. 'Shh,' he whispered as he parted the curtains to his tent with his elbow. 'Enough of words.'

And so she fell silent. Except for the tiny mewls of pleasure that escaped unbidden when his mouth descended once more, this time to plunder hers with an even greater hunger.

He was right, she thought in one fleeting moment of clarity amidst a whirl of sensation. Why ruin this perfect moment, this perfect night? For maybe, just maybe, he wouldn't even know.

He lowered her to a bed, plush and welcoming, and richly adorned with pillows of satin and brocades in Bedouin shades, a combination rich in texture and colour. A lamp at the bedside was turned low, casting shadows around the room, turning colours deeper, accenting both the blue-black of his whiskered cheeks and the glint in his sapphire eyes.

He looked massive standing above her, tall and impossibly good-looking, and she caught her breath at the look in his eyes, at the raw desire she saw there.

Desire for her.

Desire that ramped up her own need tenfold.

It was surreal that after everything between them, after all the years and the angst and the pain of coming together again, this day had finally come. It would only be for a night. She knew it couldn't last. But neither did she know what she had done to deserve this moment.

'Beautiful,' he growled, and it wasn't just the word or the gravel-rich tones of his voice that moved her, but the way his eyes, dark with desire, drank her in, and the rigid set of his jaw and throat, as though it was taking every bit of control he possessed not to throw himself on top of her.

Time lost all meaning as he stood there. It could have been just a minute. It could have been an hour. But it was a moment of connection she recognised, a moment that had been inevitable from the very first moment they'd set eyes on each other.

I do love him, she acknowledged, in that one crystal-clear moment. And this time there was no fear to accompany it, no shame, just a rolling tide of heat that coursed through her. For she was with Rafiq, and it was right.

He smiled then, a tight, hard-won smile, as if he enjoyed the way her body reacted to him, before he pulled the pristine robe over his shoulders and tossed it unceremoniously aside.

Her brain shortened.

Her mouth went dry.

For he was magnificent.

Once upon a time she'd known him, ridden horses with him, swum with him. He'd been fit, his body muscled and toned, but he'd been a youth then, still a teenager. Whereas now...

Now he was a man in his prime. He had the same rich golden skin that she remembered, but the shoulders were broader, and dark hair patterned in whorls across his chest, circled his navel and sent an arrow pointing down his hard-packed stomach before disappearing under the band of his boxer shorts.

She swallowed.

His *massively distended* boxer shorts.

She shuddered, suddenly unsure, a new fear assailing her even as the prospect of taking him—*that*—inside her body thrilled her at some primeval level she couldn't quite comprehend. She wanted him—oh yes, she wanted him—but what if she couldn't? What if he was too big?

'Rafiq,' she started breathily, caught between nervousness and heady excitement, her voice no more than a gasp as she contemplated the impossible. 'I'm afraid.'

And he smiled the smile of a man who was used to being complimented. 'There's no need to be afraid,' he said, before he placed one knee on the bed beside her, slipping the sandals from her feet and sliding one hand up her foot from toe to ankle, so slowly, so intimately, that she almost cried out with the sheer pleasure of his touch.

Pleasure or need? Both, she decided, as he trailed a line along her calf through the silk of her gown, the heat from his fingers warming her flesh and igniting fires under her skin as his voice washed warm like velvet over her. 'I know it's been a while, but it's like riding a bicycle. You never forget.'

Assuming you'd ever learned. Should she tell him outright? And then his long fingers swept over her thigh, his thumb perilously close to touching her *there*, and the sensations he generated, the raw hunger that met her touch, made her think that maybe she might just be able to bluff her way through it after all. The flesh she'd hitherto been so ashamed of, the flesh she'd numbed into non-existence for so long, was willing, even if she herself was weak.

The bones at her hip had never felt so special, nor had the dip in her waist felt so curved as his hand slipped past, and she was breathless now, breathless with his slow ascent, and through it all he watched her, blue eyes on black, his smile like a victor about to enjoy the spoils. And then his thumb grazed one tight breast and she cried out with the unexpected and unfamiliar pleasure, her spine arching against the bed. He dropped himself over her and smiled. 'You see? Like riding a bicycle.'

She blinked up at him and her brain shorted, with not a clue why he should be talking about bicycles, knowing only that Rafiq's mouth was descending again, knowing that he would kiss her again and that it had already been too long since the last one.

The touch of lips, the nuzzle of noses, the rasp of whiskered skin against her cheek—how could such simple things feel so good? Even the heat emanating from the man hovering over her warmed her soul and pleasured her senses, driving her need.

She mewed and sighed as sensation rippled into sensation,

her fingers curling into the coverlet as he kissed her throat, suckled at her flesh, turned her inside out with desire. Why had nobody warned her it could be like this?

And then his mouth ventured lower, his lips closing over a breast, his tongue circling her aching nipple. Two thin layers of cloth were no barrier. The shockwaves were spearing down to her core.

Or had she just forgotten how good it could be to feel?

All those years when she'd buried everything. Her needs. Her desires. And especially her memories of a dark-haired youth who'd made her feel like a woman. Beautiful. Desirable. The woman he had promised not to take until a wedding night that would never be.

Even then he had set her alight with his touch, just the trail of his fingers down her arm, the feel of his hand in hers. Even then, in her youth, she'd known how good one special man could make her feel.

One special man.

That was Rafiq.

And he was here now.

She shrugged off her inexperience as Rafiq peeled away the layers of her shame and his hot mouth devoured her breasts, her stomach, and then moved back to suckle at her rock-hard nipples. Gasping, breathless, she let her useless hands find a purpose after all. She reached for him, found him, felt the jolt that moved through him as her fingers spread, taking the measure of his chest and sliding down his sides before letting her fingers trail back up the sleek wall of muscled flesh.

Air whooshed out of him as her fingers found the tight nubs of his nipples, hard as pebbles on the beach, and flicked over them with her thumb, and there was something empowering knowing that she had caused his reaction. Oh, he felt so good—

the sculpted planes of his chest rippling under her hands so perfect! She thought briefly about all those wasted years when she'd felt nothing but humiliation. Nothing but shame. Then she thought fleetingly about all those wasted minutes and seconds when she'd been lying here, too tentative to reach out and touch the man above her who was making her feel again. Making her blood fizz.

Wasted years. Wasted moments, every one of them.

She would waste no more.

Starting now.

Drowning under his kisses, she let her palms follow the sculpted arch of his back, finding the band of his boxers and pressing her fingernails beneath, her fingers tracing the line that circled his firm hips, until her hands were almost between them and the only place to go was down…

A hand snared her wrist.

'Not so fast.' She blinked up at him, wondering if she'd done something wrong, wondering if she'd just revealed the extent of her inexperience, to see eyes wild with want, his features taut with control. 'If you're going to touch me there, I really need you out of that dress.'

He was just the man to peel it from her. He rocked back on his knees, his hands at her ankles before they started the slow ascent once more, each leg getting the special treatment, skimming the fabric of her gown from her skin and gathering it at his wrists as he went.

He peeled the silken fabric away, uncovering her, exposing her inch by slow inch, and yet still his eyes never strayed from hers. When his thumbs grazed her inner thighs, and her muscles clenched and jerked, he simply smiled with satisfaction—and she understood, because of the moment her hands had grazed his nipples and he had started, and she had realised the power of her own touch.

He wanted her to feel good. He delighted in it. There was no need to feel apprehensive or afraid. She was in safe hands.

She lifted her hips before he had to ask, allowing the swish of bunched stone-encrusted silk to slide past her until his hands gathered at her waist, his thumbs performing lazy circles around her navel.

Lazy circles that felt anything but. Lazy circles that turned her insides to jelly.

He leaned over then, pressed his mouth to the physical reminder of her birth and kissed it reverently before he rose. 'We need to get this off,' he muttered, sounding strangely troubled, his voice as thick as the sinking sands that had swallowed her car. And then leaned down and drew her into his embrace as he kissed her again, and she let him draw the garment over her head.

She heard a sound like a waterfall as the bejewelled gown pooled on the rug, felt one brief moment of regret for its unfair fate—and just as swiftly forgot it as Rafiq chose that same moment to look down upon her body.

'I thought you were beautiful last night, in the moonlight, emerging from the sea,' he said. 'But tonight you are perfection.'

Her heart swelled in her chest. She was so close to tears—but tears of euphoria and not of sadness. For he was a god and he was calling her perfect! She thanked whatever kind fortune had brought her this moment, this night. For she would remember it for ever.

He lowered himself over her, so that their bodies met length to delicious length, their mouths enmeshed, their tongues tangled, their bodies skin to skin apart from the underwear they both wore—the underwear Rafiq was already intent on removing. He kissed the line of her bra straps, sliding them from her shoulders in the process. And then, with a skilful and, the reason for which she didn't want to dwell on, he snapped open the closure at her back. With a flick of his wrists, even that scrap of material was gone.

The lamplight threw crazy shadows across the room—crazy shadows that merged with the crazy ideas in her mind and the crazy feelings in her heart. She had loved Rafiq once. He had loved her. Could he love her again?

Then his hot tongue circled one nipple, sending spears of pleasure down to her very core, and she didn't care what he felt.

She loved him. She wanted him. He was here now.

That was enough.

His hot mouth was at her breasts, his teeth and tongue combining in their unmerciful assault against one tight nipple and then the other, and her spine was arching with the delicious pleasure, so that she was barely aware of the downward slide of her underwear, or of his.

Until his tongue circled a nipple and she felt his hand cup her mound, felt his long fingers separate her, heat into molten heat, driving her head into the pillows with the sheer force of it. With the wonder of it. With the near agony and ecstasy when he zeroed in on that tight nub of nerves and circled it, the flick of a fingertip turning her inside out.

'Rafiq!' she cried, not entirely understanding what she was so desperate for, only knowing that his touch, her very delight, was suddenly her torture.

'I know,' he whispered, and he suckled at her throat on the way to reclaiming her mouth, 'I feel it too.' And he lay atop her and she felt him, naked and wanting, hard and heavy against her belly. 'I can't wait either.'

And this time her stab of fear at what was to follow was blunted by his hot kisses and the knowledge of his own desire and the hot rush of moisture between her thighs. She wanted him. That thought was paramount. She wanted him more than anything in the world, wanted to feel him inside her. Deep inside her, where her body ached so very much to receive him. And she wanted him *now*.

'Look at me,' she heard him urge. 'Open your eyes.' And, when finally she had complied, 'Keep them open. I want to see your eyes when you come.'

He'd sheathed himself and was already between her legs, his thickness nudging at her slick entrance, and her breath hitched, the internal muscles she'd never known already participating, trying to draw him in to their own dance of seduction.

She was burning with need, burning with fire, and the weight of him was heavy against her flesh. Heavy and yet compelling. And still she could feel his control, his tension, as the muscles bunched in his arms around her head, as his body seemed drawn tighter than a bowstring, waiting to release the arrow.

And she looked for him then—because if he was going to see her come, she wanted the very same. Their eyes connected, fused, and the circuit was complete.

And then he moved.

His hips swayed against hers, once and then again. She felt the push and the power, his masculine force against her feminine core, and feared for a moment the impossibility of it ever happening. But he must have read her panic in her eyes, because he slowed and kissed her. Slowly, thoroughly, soul-deep. So deep she melted into him even as he angled her higher.

She looked up at him in that moment and loved him. With her eyes and her heart and her very soul. Loved him for waiting, for hesitating, and for not rushing her. Loved him for the youth he had been. Loved him for the man he was now.

Loved him as he drove into her in one mind-blowing lunge that had her screaming his name.

It couldn't be possible. Rafiq was immobilised, buried to the hilt inside her. Buried tight.

Surely it wasn't possible.

And she opened her eyes and looked up at him, a tear sliding from each eye and scampering for her hair, wonder and astonishment meeting his questioning gaze, telling him that it was.

'Please,' she pleaded, her voice husky with sex. 'Don't stop. I want you.'

And even inside her he felt himself swell against the press of her tight, slick walls.

She was a virgin. *Had been* a virgin.

'Please,' she repeated impatiently, tilting her hips in a way far more persuasive than any words.

One hundred questions raced through his mind, one hundred answers eluded him, and yet he knew this was no time for explanations. The moment he had waited for in vain so many years ago, the moment he had been cheated of, was now his. Totally, exclusively, gloriously his.

And she *was* glorious.

With her black hair splayed across his pillow, her breasts firm and hard-tipped, the sensual curve of waist to hip where they joined.

She was his. *Only his.* And he was glad.

He moved inside her, testing her depths, and she cried out—this time in pleasure—her head pressing into the pillow, before he slowly withdrew, her fingers curling into the bedcover even as her inexperienced muscles clung desperately to him, as if afraid he would not return. She didn't know him well, for there was no way he could not.

He could take it slowly, in deference to her inexperience. He could try to be gentle. But something told him she wanted neither slow nor gentle. Whatever had been the problem in her marriage, she didn't want pity. She wanted him, all of him, and she would have him.

Poised at the very brink, his body screaming for completion, he wrapped her long legs around his back. 'Look at me,' he said. 'Feel me.'

And then he lunged into her again, felt her stretch and hug around him, and recognised somewhere amidst the shower of stars in his brain that he was a fool for even thinking he might be able to go slowly, for there was not a chance.

Each lunge became more desperate, each withdrawal became more fleeting, and she moved with him in the dance, welcomed him, clung to him, driving him mad with the demands of her own pulsing body.

Until her pulses turned into red-hot conflagration and she came apart around him, her eyes wild and wanton, and it was so satisfying that he had no choice but to follow her into the raging inferno.

'Did I hurt you?' She was bundled in his arms, their bodies spooned together, as slowly they wended their way down from that mountaintop.

'Only for just a second,' she admitted hesitantly. 'But I didn't mind. It was wonderful.'

'It *was* wonderful,' he agreed, remembering just how good as he pressed his lips into her hair, breathing her in deep for the space of three long breaths before asking the question that had been uppermost in his mind.

'Why didn't you tell me?'

CHAPTER ELEVEN

SHE stilled in his arms, suddenly so rigid it was a wonder she didn't snap. So he had worked it out. She'd wondered when he'd hesitated, been afraid he would stop. And yet blessedly, thankfully, he hadn't stopped, hadn't expressed surprise or demanded explanation. Instead he'd taken her to a place she'd never been, had shown her a world where she was a stranger, a place of miracles and wonder and magical new sensations.

But he must have been curious. The question had been bound to come. She swallowed back on the lump in her throat and sniffed.

'Ten years of marriage and still a virgin. It's not exactly the kind of thing you want to admit to anyone.' Her voice sounded flat, even to her own ears, and the wonder and delight of her previous words was long gone. 'It's not exactly the kind of thing you can be proud of.' Her voice caught, half a hiccup, on that last word, and she jammed her eyes together to stop the memories and the tears that accompanied them. But the pictures remained; the endless humiliation persisted.

'Sera?' She felt herself tugged around to face him. 'Look at me, Sera.' Reluctantly she prised open her flooded eyes. 'You were wasted on him—do you understand me? A man would be a fool not to want to make love to you. Hussein was that fool.'

But her lips remained tightly clenched. Rafiq didn't understand. Hussein had wanted to, had even been desperate to, she was sure. Why else make her strip in front of him and make her perform like some cheap nightclub dancer as he tugged on himself futilely? And why else would he have been so angry, so bitter, when nothing worked?

'He said I wasn't beautiful enough or enticing enough. He said it was my fault that we would never have children—that because I was so undesirable my womb would remain forever empty.'

Blood heated in his veins, reached boiling point in the time it took to take his next breath. 'Hussein told you that? But you didn't believe him? You couldn't have believed him?'

She shrugged. It wasn't just because of Hussein, but there was no reason to tell Rafiq that. He had discovered she was a virgin and she felt she owed him some kind of explanation. But there was no need to tell him anything else. No need to reveal any more humiliating truths.

'Why else could he not make love to his own wife? His own wife, Rafiq! For ten years. Why else would he say such things if they were not true?'

'Because he was using you as an excuse for his own inadequacies! I swear that if Hussein weren't already dead, I would kill him myself.'

'Rafiq, you mustn't say that!'

'Why not? It would not be murder. He was not a man. He was barely a cockroach. So why do you rush to his defence when he fed you nothing but lies, when he brainwashed you into thinking it was you with the problem?'

'But you were not there. You don't know——'

'I know this. That you have no problem, Sera. You are the most desirable woman I have ever met and I have had no trouble wanting you from the moment I saw you outside my mother's apartments.'

He kissed the last of her tears from her eyes, pushed her hair behind her ear with her fingers and followed the movement down her neck to shoulder and below, cupping one breast in his hand. She trembled, her breast already swelling, her nipple budding hard against his palm.

'Why is it so hard to believe, Sera? You are a beautiful woman. A desirable woman. Can you not see what you do to me?'

She felt the nudge of him against her belly and looked down, gasping to see him already swelling into life again. A sizzle of anticipation coursed through her. 'You want to do it again?'

And he smiled. 'And again, and again, and again.'

His words shocked her, thrilled her, confused her. 'But I thought you… I thought this was all about revenge. Because of what you thought you'd been cheated out of. You were so angry before. You said you hated me—'

And he pulled her to him, cradling her head against his chest, aching because she was so right, and had just cause for thinking it. 'I know, and you're right. It *was* revenge in the beginning. It was a desire to get even that drove me. I wanted you to accompany me to Marrash to spite you, because I could see you were afraid.' He paused, retraced his words. 'It was hate. I'd had more than a decade to do nothing but build a shrine to hatred, and I worshipped there every chance I got. Seeing you again brought the hatred back tenfold. In my own perverse way, making sure you came seemed the perfect way to punish you. I wanted you to suffer in my company if you hated it that much. But I had no idea how much I would suffer in yours, purely because of wanting you.'

She looked up at him with wide eyes. Was it possible he was telling the truth? Was it possible? 'You really did want me?'

'I never stopped wanting you,' he confessed, running his fingers through the thick black weight of her hair to cup her neck and draw her closer into his talking kiss. 'As you know I want you now. If you feel ready.'

Her lips tingled as she felt his words on her lips, as his teeth nipped at her for an answer. 'If I feel ready?'

'I know you might feel too tender.'

Parts of her did feel tender. Deliciously, lusciously tender. But definitely ready. 'Make love with me, Rafiq.' *Make love with me and blot out the memories of Hussein and his cronies and the men who looked at me as if I was dirt.* 'Make me come apart again.'

Three more times she'd come apart before, utterly exhausted, she'd fallen asleep in his arms. Three more times he'd marvelled at her responsive body, at the way she fitted him so perfectly. She stirred in her sleep and sighed, nestling back into him like a kitten.

But, unusually for Rafiq after a night of sex, sleep eluded him. He lay there in the dark, listening to the sound of her breathing, slow and even, wondering what it was that felt different.

He still wanted her. That felt different. Usually he could discard a woman as easily as he'd picked her up, his desire slaked. But Sera? How many times before his interest waned now that he had had her?

They would be back at the palace tomorrow. He would go back to doing the job he was supposed to be doing—supporting his soon-to-be-crowned brother. Sera would go back to playing companion to his mother.

Sera, who had never slept with anyone but him before.

A gentle breeze stirred up from the desert sands—a warm, unsettling breeze that whispered around the tent, rustling around the edges and whistling low through the tiny gaps.

Sera slept on—despite the steadily building wind and the flapping of canvas somewhere outside, despite the noises of his own mind that were too loud to let him sleep.

And then the coronation would be upon them, and Kareef

would be King. His duty here would be done and he would be free to return to Australia.

Why did that thought suddenly leave him cold? And he looked down at the woman nestled into his shoulder and knew.

It would be justice in a way to leave her cold now that he'd had her. He could walk away, abandon her just as she'd done to him all those years ago. And nobody would blame him.

But he didn't want that. Whatever this was—this obsession he'd had with her ever since he'd arrived, this need to have her, to possess her—he didn't want it to end just yet. Maybe he should talk to Kareef. There might be something he could do here, to give him a reason to stay a few days longer. After all, his business was fine. It wasn't as if he needed to rush back.

Something crashed outside, blown over by the wind, and the woman in his arms stirred, her sleepy eyes blinking in the first grey fingers of dawn. She smiled that secret smile he'd so missed when she saw him, and stretched, pushing deliciously against him as she arched her back.

'Good morning,' he growled, kissing her tenderly on her forehead. 'How do you feel?'

'Excellent,' she said, sliding one hand over his belly, her fingers stretched wide. 'How do *you* feel?' And then she encountered him and answered her own question, following it with a short, 'Oh…'

Not that she took her hand away. For the first time she did a little tentative exploration of her own, while his hardness danced and bucked under her inquisitive fingers. Rafiq was forced to grit his teeth as she tried and failed to complete a circle around him, before deciding that stroking him up and down was a more satisfying option. She flicked her thumb over the moist end and it was his turn to gasp.

'So smooth,' she said in awe, her teeth at her bottom lip. 'Like satin. Do you think…?'

'Do I think what?' Rafiq groaned, only a few short seconds shy of forgetting *how* to think.

Her cheeks flushed dark. 'I liked it when you flipped me over that time. Do you think it would work if this time *I* started on top?'

'I think,' he said, grinding the words out between his teeth, 'that would work just fine.'

She straddled him, and the sight of her over him, her breasts firm and dusky, nipples peaked, her black hair in riotous disarray over her shoulders and her gold-skinned body the perfect hourglass, more curvaceous and beautiful than any statue, was nearly enough to bring him undone. She took him in both hands, lifting herself to guide him to her entrance, and he wanted to weep with the pleasure of it.

And then, with a sigh, she slowly lowered herself, and he watched as he felt himself disappear deep into her honeyed depths.

He closed his eyes, using his last remaining brain cell to make a decision while there was still time. He would talk to Kareef. Find any excuse. But he was *definitely* not leaving Qusay or Sera any time soon.

The return trip to Shafar was uneventful, if you didn't count the innumerable unspoken messages that passed between Rafiq and Sera, and if you didn't count the number of times one or other of them found the flimsiest excuse to touch the other, to help locate a wayward seat belt buckle, or to brush a strand of hair from the other's eyes. She was wearing the sunset-coloured gown today, and the colour suited her even more than last night's ocean-blue—not that she'd actually worn that one for long. If he played his cards right tonight, and managed to shoehorn Sera out of his mother's apartments as he intended, this gown would no doubt meet the same fate.

He could hardly wait.

The trip back felt much quicker, and it seemed hardly any

time at all before they were through the desert and once again eating up the wide highway as they neared Shafar.

Rafiq would have preferred them to stay another night at the beach encampment, but the dawn wind had blown itself out and come to nothing, and the day that had followed the dawn was still and bright. Besides, the coronation was tomorrow. Missing a state banquet was one thing. Missing his brother's coronation would be inexcusable. But he wasn't looking forward to their return. The palace would be heaving with preparations, the walls bulging with visitors and guests, and he cared for none of it. He was pleased for his brother, but he did not really feel part of the celebrations, more an interested onlooker. The only person he really wanted to be with right now was here, in this car, the one who had so aptly labelled him the tourist prince.

So it would not hurt to play tourist a little while longer. His mother would approve of his staying longer, at least. She could hardly disapprove of his relationship with Sera—she had practically forced them together after all. Plus, if Tahir ever bothered to make an appearance, it would be an opportunity for all three brothers to catch up properly.

But his plans to run the idea past Kareef when they arrived at the palace would have to be deferred.

Akmal greeted them in the buzzing forecourt with the news that there was still no sign of Tahir, and that Kareef had taken himself down to Qais for the running of the Qais Cup. The fact that it apparently also had something to do with tonight's wedding of Jasmine, Kareef's former lover, surprised Rafiq— although Sera seemed strangely unaffected by the news.

'I thought from what you were saying that Jasmine was a friend of yours,' he said, as they retrieved their personal belongings from the car.

'She is.'

'Then how is it that you aren't going to her wedding?'

'Maybe I don't enjoy seeing a friend forced to marry someone she doesn't love.'

And the way the shutters slammed down over her features, as if she was trying to shut out something she'd rather forget, told him it was true. He grabbed her hand across the seat as she reached for her purse. 'You never loved him at all, did you?'

Her eyes didn't lift from the upholstery. 'There was only one man I ever loved.'

And before he had a chance to digest what she had said, let alone work out how to reply, she'd slipped her fingers from his and disappeared in a glide of sunset-coloured silk into the palace.

'Did everything at Marrash go to your satisfaction, Your Highness?' asked Akmal, who had suddenly reappeared at his elbow.

Rafiq's eyes were still on the doorway Sera had disappeared into. 'Very well, thank you, Akmal.' *On all counts.* Except one… He swung his head around. 'Although I'm afraid we lost one of the cars.'

'It broke down?' The older man looked sceptical.

Rafiq grimaced. 'More like got bogged down. The last time I saw it, it was up to the windows in sand.'

'Sinking sands!' Akmal's eyes opened wide, and for the first time Rafiq saw the unflappable Akmal, the man who oversaw the goings-on of an entire palace with the calm confidence of a born leader, actually look shocked—as if the prospect of losing one of Qusay's princes was clearly not on his agenda. 'I will speak to the drivers. I must apologise—it is unthinkable that something like that should happen.'

Rafiq put his hand to his wiry shoulder. 'They weren't driving. It was my fault, Akmal. But we are all safe. It ended well—apart from the car, that is.'

The vizier bowed slightly, and regained his calm demeanour. ' am pleased to hear that.'

'Oh, and Akmal?' he said, suddenly remembering something else. 'I need you to arrange something as soon as possible. But first, do you know if my mother is in the palace today?' The older man nodded. 'Good. Perhaps you might pass word that I'll visit her after we've had our chat.'

Rafiq allowed himself a smile as he slung his overnight bag over his shoulder, waving away the offers of assistance.

Given Kareef was away, once his meeting with Akmal was finished there was little other choice left to him but to visit his mother. And if visiting his mother meant that he might also run into Sera, all the better.

An hour later, the Sheikha greeted him with a smile and a song in her voice. 'My son, you are home. And how did it go in Marrash? You must tell me everything.'

Not a chance. He had no doubt she had already extracted what relevant details she could from Sera, and now it was his turn, so she could see if the pieces matched. It was a game they were playing, and who was he to throw the board into the air? At least until he knew exactly how much she knew...

'It went well, Mother,' he said, trying to deflect any underlying questions with an easygoing answer meant to show he had nothing to hide. The last thing he needed his mother knowing was that he had slept with Sera. *Several times.* And intended to sleep with her again. *Several times.*

'And you have your contract?'

'We made a deal, yes.'

She clapped her freshly hennaed hands together in delight. 'You did? How wonderful! This calls for a celebration.' The ubiquitous coffee pot made another appearance, and while his mother was busy pouring, Rafiq was busy checking out the doors. Which one led to Sera? Where was she?

He was about to take his cup when he remembered the small package he had brought. 'I brought you a gift from Marrash.

he said, handing it over. 'Actually from Abizah, an old woman who refused to take payment. A gift for you, she said.'

'For me? Thank you.' His mother took the package, as delighted as a schoolgirl. 'And thanks to Abizah.'

'It's just a trinket,' he warned.

'It's beautiful,' his mother exclaimed, holding the tiny lamp up high, letting the encrusted gems catch the light. 'It's perfect! Thank you.'

'Sera chose it. She said you would like it.' He looked around. 'Where *is* Sera?'

His mother put the gift down, took a sip of her coffee, and looked nowhere in particular in the process. 'I thought you might be more comfortable without her presence here. The last two days must have been difficult for you both.'

'Most considerate,' he replied, hooded-eyed, and sipped from his own cup. 'But unnecessary. As it happens, Sera and I have come to an—amicable arrangement. In fact…' he coughed '…Sera is the one who negotiated the deal.'

'Sera did that? Well, didn't I tell you that you would need a guide?'

'You did, and you were right. I couldn't have done it without her. She won the contract all by herself.'

'Did she now?' the Sheikha asked, clearly more delighted than surprised, and Rafiq could see she was already settling against her cushions for a long Q&A session. 'She didn't tell me that. How exactly did she do it?'

Rafiq coughed again. 'Just as you said might be the case, Sera was asked to negotiate with the women, of course.'

'Of course,' said his mother with an I-told-you-so shrug. 'So what did she do to ensure you the deal? I told you there were others interested. I'm surprised the tribespeople made up their minds so quickly.'

He hesitated, wondering if he wanted to reveal everything,

but then it was a contract, the terms would soon be known far and wide, and then his mother would wonder why he hadn't just come clean and told her in the first place. It wasn't as if he had anything to hide.

'Sera picked up on their being disappointed about it being too late to use the fabric they had sent down in the coronation. To sweeten the offer I was prepared to make, she suggested that at my wedding my bride will wear a gown made of their best golden fabric, for the eyes of the world to see.'

His mother's blue-grey eyes grew wide as she drew herself up straighter, and Rafiq was in no doubt that Sera had chosen not to share this particular snippet of news with her. To protect him from his mother's over-active imagination? Or herself?

'But you're never getting married. At least, that's what you told me. Have you changed your mind?'

He had said that. He'd meant it. And he hadn't changed his mind—although right now he just couldn't summon the same level of absolute certainty. 'I'll have the lawyers look over the terms, see if there's something else we can't offer them instead. It's too late for the coronation, but no doubt Kareef will have to marry soon…'

But even as he said the words, a vision formed unbidden in his mind, of a black-haired, kohl-rimmed dark-eyed woman in a robe spun with gold and laced with emeralds, and he wondered where the image had come from—because there was no way *that* woman was marrying Kareef. So why…?

He barely heard the door open, and his mother's exclamation was just a spike in his thoughts until he caught her sudden movement as she uncharacteristically jumped to her feet. He glanced around to see what the problem was—only to see Sera standing inside the door, her eyes wild and wet, her skin an unnatural shade of grey.

CHAPTER TWELVE

DESPITE his mother's head start, Rafiq had swooped her into his arms in a heartbeat. 'Sera, what's wrong? What's happened?'

His mother looked on, asking the same questions herself, but with more than a tinge of curiosity mingled with the concern. He couldn't care less about his mother's curiosity right now. All he knew was that Sera was hurting.

'What is it?' he said. 'Tell me. Let me make it right.'

'You can't,' Sera replied, her head rocking from side to side in his swaying arms. 'No one can fix it. She hates me.' And then, in a hollow breath, 'She will always hate me.'

And from his mother came the unfamiliar sound of air sucking over teeth. 'Cerak has had the nerve to show her face here, at the palace?'

'She has an invitation, she claims,' Sera assured her, the colour returning to her cheeks, though she was still clinging to Rafiq's arms. 'There is no way she would miss the social event of the decade.'

'Who is this woman and what did she do to you?' Rafiq demanded, impatient with his own lack of knowledge, feeling excluded from the conversation. His voice growled with his dissatisfaction. 'What did she say?'

And Sera's beautiful dark eyes shut down, her face as bleak

as the deepest, coldest winter's night. 'She said that I had poisoned her son. That he would not be dead but for me, a barren woman with a poisoned womb, who had been like poison to his very soul.' And her tears came, at first silently, her body buckling against his with the pain, but then giving way to sound as her sobs found voice.

And even as he held her, even as he comforted her, his anger boiled and raged inside him. *Hussein's mother.* He turned to his own mother then, his desire to find this woman and ram home a few home truths about her precious son paramount. 'Where will I find this witch?'

'No, Rafiq,' said his mother, putting one hand to his forearm and one to Sera's hair. 'I will find Akmal and ensure the woman leaves immediately. You are needed here, with Sera.'

She was at the door, almost gone, when he called to her. 'Make sure she is told, when they find her, that there is recorded in history just the one virgin birth, and that if she dared to look more closely she would find that any poison was the product of her own fetid womb.'

His mother did not blink. She looked from Rafiq to the woman nestled against his chest and nodded, before slipping silently from the room.

'You told her,' Sera said much later, after he had carried her to his room and laid her down on his wide bed, after he had kissed her hurt away with a thousand tiny kisses as he stripped her bare, after making slow, deliberate love to her. 'With that message for Cerak you told your mother about us.'

And he shrugged as he ran one finger down her arm, relishing the way she shivered into his touch, her glorious dusky nipples peaking once more. 'She would have found out soon enough. She was already wondering when you didn't reel from my arms.'

'Yes, of course.'

He leaned over, unable to resist, his tongue circling that budded temptation, 'Besides, even if that hug had never happened she would have put two and two together when she found out I was planning on staying a few extra days and spending them and the nights that followed in your company.'

A pause. 'You're staying longer?'

He heard the delighted note in her voice, how it rose at the end, her words delivered just a fraction faster, and it pleased him. 'I was thinking about it.' He targeted the second nipple, feeling spoiled for choice, loving the way she gasped as he suckled, drawing her in tight. 'But I changed my mind.'

'Oh.' Exit delighted note.

He slid first one leg between hers and then the other, pressing his lips to her softly curved belly and then lower, his hand sliding down, parting her, circling that tight bundle of nerve-endings that knew only his touch and which was guaranteed to have her arching her spine.

'I had a better idea.'

He dipped his head, working his teeth around a nipple, gnawing, nipping, laving with his tongue while his hand worked his magic below. She was panting now, her breath coming in ragged, frantic breaths as her fingers clutched at his hair, his shoulders, her nails digging into his skin. But some part of her brain must have still been functioning.

'Which was?' she asked. And he had to switch gears in his mind to work out what he'd said before.

Although his first priority right now was not with words but with actions. She was ready for him, and he could not wait. He sheathed himself in an instant and waited at her very cusp, his muscles bunched and readied as he sought her eyes. Only when he had them did he answer. 'I want you to come back to Sydney with me.'

Her eyes opened wide. With pleasure? Or shock? But the

time for conversation was long gone, his ability to converse gone the same way, his focus required elsewhere.

He lunged into her, filling her in that heated way he did, and her mind swirled to get hold of the words he'd uttered, battling to hold onto them even as he lunged again, deeper this time, faster, more ferocious. And then his mouth was on hers, his slick body bucking into hers again and again, and she was lost. She spun away, or so it seemed, wild and out of control and weightless, his cry of triumph her trophy.

'Come back with me,' he urged through breath still uneven, after they'd collapsed together, heavy-limbed and exhausted.

'I can't,' she replied, confused and unsure, and not knowing what it was he actually was asking of her, what it meant. 'Your mother—'

'You cannot stay now. Everyone will know the truth—that you have been with me. In Australia it would not matter, but here in Qusay...'

She put a hand to her head. He didn't have to finish the sentence. He was right. Here she would pay for her recklessness, in sly looks and whispered innuendo. Hussein's mother alone would guarantee there was a steady stream of gossip about her failed daughter-in-law after the humiliation of her ejection from the palace. But Australia?

'Besides,' he continued, pushing himself up on one arm, using the other to emphasise his points, 'there is nothing for you here. Nothing but the ghosts of your past. And you will love Australia, Sera. There are deserts and endless skies, like here, but there are snow-capped mountains and tropical islands, and rainforests and cities that sprawl along the coast.'

It sounded wonderful, and she longed to see it all, especially at Rafiq's side, but still she didn't understand, didn't want to read too much into his offer. It didn't mean what her heart wanted it to mean. It couldn't. Not given this was the man who had so recently professed his hatred for her. But maybe he didn't hate her so much any more—at least not when they were in bed. Or maybe that was how he'd redirected all that energy…

'You mean, like a holiday?'

'Live with me! I have a house in Sydney that overlooks the cliffs and the sea. You should see the surf when it storms, Sera, it is spectacular—like the passion unleashed in you when you come apart in my arms.'

'But I don't understand what you're saying. I thought… You said before that you would never marry me. Yet now you are asking me to live with you?'

He raked a hand through his hair. He was struggling to make sense of it too, she could tell.

'How could I ever contemplate marriage after what happened?' His eyes appealed to hers, the pain of her betrayal laid bare in their blue depths, and then he reached out and laced her fingers in his. 'But I didn't understand. I thought you wanted to marry him. I thought you wanted a rich husband and the lavish lifestyle to go with it. But I was wrong. I couldn't see past my pain. I understand now why you acted as you did back then. I understand you had no choice. I want you, Sera, and if having you in my bed has shown me anything, it's that whatever this attraction is between us isn't going away any time soon. A few nights longer here won't be enough. I want you in my bed at home.'

His words swirled and eddied in her mind. She was scared she was imagining it all. She was almost too scared to breathe.

'Anyway,' he continued with a shrug, his thumb making lazy circles on the back of her hand, 'when it all boils down to it, live with me or marry me—what's the real difference? Maybe we *should* get married. Then you can make a start on those six children you always wanted.'

'What are you talking about? You said you'd never marry me. *Never!*'

'That was before. Before I knew the truth. My father treated you abysmally—everyone treated you abysmally—and I was so wrong. Why not marry me and let me make up for the wrongs of the past?'

It was too much to take in, and her mind was spinning with the possibilities. *Marriage to Rafiq. Bearing his children.* Her heart thudded against her ribs, echoed loud in her veins, his words her every fantasy come true. Did he understand what he was offering? What an unbelievable gift he was holding out to her?

Could it mean the impossible?

Was there a chance his love for her had been revived after the crushing weight of years of hatred?

It was crazy, just crazy to imagine it. Crazy to think that after all this time they could be together, could wipe away those painful years and start over. But if he loved her…? Maybe it could work. But he hadn't said he loved her, had he? He'd given her no inkling that love was any part of this crazy plan. No inkling at all.

'It doesn't work like that, Rafiq. You don't just marry someone and have their babies because you enjoy the sex. What if you change your mind in a week or a month? What if you've had enough by then and we're stuck together? It doesn't make sense.'

He didn't understand it either. He only knew that he wasn't about to let Sera go. Ever. And if the best way to do that was to marry her, he'd do it. Gladly. And then he hit on the perfect way to convince her.

'Don't you see?' he added, his eyes suddenly alive with excitement as he sprang up on the bed. 'It makes perfect sense. The Marrashis want a royal marriage. We'll provide them with one. Save all the legal hassles of renegotiating the contract terms. It's the sensible thing to do.'

The contract. Sera felt her fledgling hopes take a dive. Rafiq was nothing if not a consummate businessman. Of course it would all be about the contract. Of course he didn't love her.

The Marrashis had tied his hands. He could marry or face some kind of renegotiation and possibly risk the entire contract in the process. Marrying her was clearly the lesser of two evils. *Sensible.*

'Sera, what do you think? Isn't it perfect?'

Perfect? Nowhere near.

'Aren't you taking a lot for granted?' She had to say something. She could not just let him steamroller her into this—not when it was for the wrong reasons. 'You seem to assume I'd be happy to marry you.'

He frowned. 'Would it be such a chore…?' He ran his hand down her side, a featherlight touch all the way from her shoulder to one knee that made her quiver. 'Putting up with me every night?'

'But it's not just about sex, surely?'

And his eyes took on a glacial hue, as if he was annoyed she was not falling in easily with his ever so *sensible* plan. 'Who was it who came up with that condition, Sera? Who was it who led the Marrashis to believe there would be a wedding and that it would be mine? Who had those women believing that you would be that bride?'

She swallowed and looked away. 'I didn't tell them that—'

'You might as well have, because that's what they expect. You owe me, Sera. Marry me. It's the least you can do. Say yes, before I am forced to command you.'

He was serious. He was actually serious. The concept of merely living together was forgotten. Now he was demanding she marry him as if he was calling in a debt. She swallowed down on her disappointment.

Maybe it wasn't all bad. Okay, so he might not love her—she could hardly expect that from a man who had so recently expressed his hatred of her—but he did want her. Of that she had no doubt. Could she settle for marriage with Rafiq, bearing his children, loving him, even knowing he didn't love her?

And she looked up into the waiting eyes, the beautiful blue eyes in the beautiful chiselled face of the man who had a place in her heart and her soul for ever, whether or not he loved her, now or ever, and she knew her answer.

'You don't have to command me. I'll do it. I'll marry you.'

Coronation morning dawned bright and beautiful. Rafiq knew this because he'd been awake and had watched the silvery-grey morning light spear through the drapes and turn Sera's gold-tinged skin to satin. He'd lain there, watching her sleep on a pillow of her own black hair, the curve of her long lashes resting on her cheek, her lush mouth an invitation, her lips, slightly parted.

When would he get sick of looking at her? When would he get sick of making love to her? Never, if the hunger he felt for her even now was any indication. Never, if she remained so responsive to his touch.

Sleep had confirmed last night's brainwave. Marriage would solve everything. Sera would be safe away from here. She would be free from the ghosts of her past, able to make a new future.

But most of all she would be his.

And nothing and nobody was ever going to steal her away from him again.

He pressed his lips to hers, unable to resist their silent invitation any longer, and she stirred and stretched into sleepy wakefulness so deliciously that he could not resist kissing her again, finally groaning as he pulled away, knowing there was no time for them to make love this morning.

'I'm having breakfast with Kareef before the coronation, and from there we'll go to the ceremony together. I will have Akmal assign you a seat next to mine, and I will join you there after the official entrance.'

Sleep slid from her eyes like a coverlet slipping from a bed, exposing emotion so naked he almost flinched. 'But I wasn't planning on going to the coronation.'

He sat back. 'Of course you are. It's Kareef's coronation. Why wouldn't you be there?'

She was shaking her head, clutching her bedclothes in front of her like a shield. 'There's no need. Or…I can stand at the back. Because you'll be right up at the front with your family. I don't need—'

He took her shrouded hands in his. 'Sera, what's wrong?'

'There's just no point. I don't need to be there, to take someone else's seat.'

'Sera, Cerak will not be there. She cannot hurt you now. She has been banished.'

But still Sera's eyes looked panicked and turbulent. 'I will go with you to Australia. Didn't I agree to that? I'll go today, if necessary. Oh, Rafiq,' she said, clutching at his shoulder, 'could we not go today? Why not leave right after the ceremony? Just slip away in all the commotion? Your plane is still here. It would be easy.'

His patience was wearing thin. Last night she'd made it seem as if marrying him would be some kind of imposition, and now she was suggesting they leave today—before the crown was barely warm on Kareef's head, before the event he'd specifically flown all the way from Australia to attend had barely concluded?

'Now you're being ridiculous. It's not as if you don't have anything to wear.' He headed for the bathroom. He'd wasted enough time on this meaningless discussion. If she'd played her cards right, they could have used their time much more productively. He turned at the door. 'This is my brother's coronation. You are going to be my wife. There will be no standing at the back. You *are* family now, and I expect you by my side. Is that understood?'

* * *

The conversation troubled him, even as he breakfasted with Kareef, even as he should have been focusing on his brother's words and his needs. But Kareef seemed strangely at odds with himself too, and uninterested in Rafiq's half-hearted talk of contracts with the tribespeople of Marrash. Or was that just because he found it hard to regain the enthusiasm for his own success after this morning's strange conversation with Sera? It was certainly not the way he intended waking up with Sera again.

News of their impending marriage would have snagged Kareef's attention, he was sure. But today was Kareef's day, and there was nothing he would do to deflect attention from that. There would be time for that announcement later. Not that Kareef didn't look as if he could do with some cheering up. Maybe if Tahir had managed to make it in time, as he'd promised? But their younger brother was nothing if not scrupulously unreliable, and, sadly, there seemed scant possibility he'd show up now.

An onshore breeze caught them as they crossed the courtyard, whipping at his robes as he walked side by side with his brother, and the cries of the crowd outside the gates interfered with his tangled thoughts. Once again he'd made the decision to don the robes of his countrymen. It was not so much to ask, he'd decided. Not so much of a stretch as he'd imagined. Maybe there were some parts of Qusay he didn't need to forget.

Sera had turned out to be one of them.

He frowned. Would she be waiting for him inside the ancient ruin? Or had whatever had been troubling her this morning swung her mind, and she was hiding somewhere in the cloistered shadows, as she'd clearly been intending?

It didn't make sense. Cerak had been taken care of. So what was her problem?

* * *

Today Sera had reluctantly chosen the peacock-blue gown from Marrash to wear. She had fingered her black *abayas* lovingly, wishing she could hide under one of those, and hopefully go unnoticed and unrecognised, but Rafiq would be upset, she knew, and already today she had angered him. And now there was colour all around her, a multitude of guests dressed in finery from one hundred nations, and still she felt achingly conspicuous as she sat in the seat Akmal had arranged for her, so close to the front that she could feel a thousand eyes at her back, a butterfly for each pair flitting inside her. She kept her own eyes to the front, not wanting to meet any of them, managing an awkward smile only when the Sheikha caught her eye. Her lover's mother! What must she think? She wished Rafiq would get here, so that she could at least hide herself against him. He had defended her against Cerak, made sure she could not hurt her again. He made her feel safe.

She took a deep breath, tried to settle her jittery stomach and cool her damp palms. Soon he would take her away from here. Far away from Qusay and the palace and any chance of running into someone from her past. She could hardly wait.

The sound of trumpets filled the air and the crowd hushed, heads swivelling around to where the official party gathered at the back. Relief quelled her flighty stomach. Rafiq would be among them. Soon he would be here. But for now she resisted the temptation of turning her head, waiting until the party had made their way almost to the front before she dared glance behind her.

Her gaze never made it to the official party. He was staring at her, the ambassador from Karakhistar, his burgundy sash stretched across a white dress shirt that looked a size too small for his spreading paunch. But it was the sneering look of contempt on his face that turned her stomach. The nervous butterflies were now massive moths, writhing in their death throes inside her. And she remembered the night when Hussein had ordered her to sit alongside the ambassador, her breasts practically spilling from the near-transparent top Hussein had insisted she wear, and how he had reached for her greedily, with pudgy fingers, thinking she was the entertainment, before Hussein had bundled him unceremoniously out—only to make her watch while he had tried and failed to achieve the same level of arousal as his guest, cursing her for her failure to stimulate him.

She dropped her head, her hand going over her mouth, sweat beading at her brow. She was so glad now that her heaving stomach was empty, that there was nothing to lose, nothing to further humiliate herself with. And suddenly Rafiq was there alongside her, his arm around her back.

'What's wrong?' he whispered, even as the voice of Akmal could be heard as the ceremony began.

'Take me away,' she managed. 'Take me away from Qusay.'

'I will,' he promised, his voice thick with questions that she could not answer, *dared not answer*, in case he changed his mind and left her here after all.

There was a stir amongst the guests, a ripple of astonishment that had heads turning once again, and a feeling that things were going off the rails. Even in the depths of her misery, Sera heard Rafiq's muttered, 'What the—?'

And she looked up, her mind not believing the picture her eyes were telling her. Jasmine? In Kareef's arms? *Kissing?*

'What's happening?' she said.

But Rafiq only scowled as Akmal uttered the fateful words, 'Kareef Al'Ramiz has renounced the throne. Long live King Rafiq!'

CHAPTER THIRTEEN

'WHAT the hell just happened in there?' Rafiq wasn't pacing the room, he was devouring it, with giant purposeful strides that ate up the carpet and spat it out again. 'Akmal, tell me—what the hell happened? One minute my brother is supposed to be crowned King, the next he is renouncing the throne. He cannot *do* that.'

'Yes, Akmal,' his mother added, sitting alongside a sick-looking Sera on a couch, 'what does it mean?'

Akmal stood, eerily composed, his hands knotted in front of him, the only one in the room who seemed to have recovered from the pandemonium of the last few minutes. 'Kareef can renounce the crown and has done so. He did that when he decided to marry Jasmine Kouri, a woman unable to bear him children.'

Rafiq was shaking his head, but there was no shutting out the crashing sound of the chains and bars of responsibility clanging shut around him. 'But I am a businessman. I am flying home to Australia tomorrow. I cannot be Qusay's king.'

'You are the second son. The first has abdicated. That makes you first in line to the throne now.' Akmal's voice was patient and deliberate as he set out the facts, each one hammering home Rafiq's fate.

'But it makes no sense,' he railed. 'I know nothing of Qusay's affairs. I have not lived here for more than a decade.' He turned to Sera then, noticed her wide eyes and still ashen skin and felt himself frown. 'Some might even call me a tourist prince…'

Instead of a smile, as he'd hoped, she winced and shrank back further into the sofa, and he remembered she'd been upset even before the ceremony. Had she known, even then, that her old friend would marry Kareef? Yet the dramatic turn of events had taken everyone by surprise, including Kareef and Jasmine, it seemed. So what was bothering her?

Akmal's steady voice hauled his attention back. 'It matters neither what you did before nor what you know. For it is written in your blood. Kareef has stepped aside and it is your place to become King.'

And even though he still shook his head, he knew Akmal was right. He had no choice. His blood had spoken. So much for his fly in, fly out visit—so much for being relaxed about being second in line for the throne, smug in the knowledge that soon Kareef would marry and provide the heirs that would distance him from the throne. Kareef had fairly and squarely dropped him right in it.

And yet how could he damn his brother for snatching this chance at happiness with the woman he had loved for ever? How could he blame him, when he knew what it was like to find that woman again after so many years—the woman of your very heart and soul?

The woman you loved.

And a wave rushed through him, a tidal wave of realisation that felt like pure light coursing through his body, finally illuminating the truth.

He loved her. *Sera.* And he would marry her. He looked at her now, huddled into the seat, and he yearned to take her into his arms and soothe away whatever pain was hurting her. Something had upset her and upset her deeply, and he needed to find out what it was.

He turned back to Akmal, hauled in a deep breath. 'I under-stand,' he said, even when his mind was still reeling from his recent discovery, still connecting the dots. 'We have a palace full of dignitaries we have already inconvenienced. How long can we wait before this coronation will proceed? There is much I must do beforehand.'

The vizier nodded, clearly pleased to see that order might once again be restored. 'No more than a few days, I am sure. Many guests were planning on staying longer to tour the emerald mines. They should not be too inconvenienced.'

'Good. And be sure, when you tell them, to say that they will see a double celebration. For they will also witness my marriage that day to Sera.'

A wail of distress, a cry of absolute agony, rent the air, and she was on her feet and at the door in a moment, her black hair swinging crazily as she hauled it open and disappeared before anyone knew what was happening.

'Sera!' he shouted, as he wrenched the door open behind her, but the passageway was empty and she was gone. He turned back to the room, confused, wondering just when it had been that he had started losing control of this day—when his world had tilted sideways and everything he'd known, everything he'd held precious, had somehow slipped out of his grasp.

'I'll find her,' his mother assured him, her hand soft on his forearm. 'You have things to discuss with Akmal.' And he blindly nodded and let her glide from the room. Let his mother talk to Sera. Let his mother soothe her fears and doubts. Because if he could be King, surely she could be Queen? After being an ambassador's wife for so many years, how hard could it be?

'Akmal,' he said, getting back to business, trying to forget Sera's impassioned cry, the tortured look on her face as she'd ed, 'have you had any luck with my other request?'

The older man nodded. 'The team arrives later today, and the procedure is scheduled for tomorrow morning.'

Rafiq sighed with relief. At least *something* in his world was going to plan.

His mother told him where he would find Sera: down the carved steps that wound their way down from the palace to the small, secluded private beach. 'Sera will talk to you there,' his mother had said, 'away from the palace and prying eyes and ears. 'She will explain.'

He didn't understand what there was to explain. She'd agreed to marry him less than twenty-four hours previously. What was there to explain—unless it was her erratic behaviour of today?

She stood at the far end of the small cove, looking out to sea as the sun settled low on the horizon, her blue robe fluttering in the breeze, her black hair lifting where the breeze caught it over her shoulders and her breasts imprinted on the fabric by the kiss of the wind. So beautiful, he thought, as he crunched his way through the warm sand of the tiny cove, and yet so very forlorn.

This beach had seen so much, he thought, wondering if that was a good omen or bad. For it was here that Queen Inas had found Zafir, the Calistan prince, washed up half-dead on the shore. It was in this place that, drunk with grief, she'd taken him for her own dead child, Xavian, and denied Rafiq's own father the crown.

This was a beach that had seen a lie perpetrated that would come majorly unstuck some three decades on. And now the unbelievable events of the past weeks had taken a more dramatic turn and the unimaginable had happened. Now, instead of his brother, Kareef, he himself would be King.

And the woman he wanted for his queen stood looking out to sea, lost and alone.

She looked around as he neared, and again he was struck b

her pallor, and the look of dread that filled her eyes. 'What is it?' he asked, wanting to take her in his arms, but she held him away and he had to settle for taking her hand, and even that slipped from his fingers as she turned to walk along the shore. 'Sera, what's wrong?'

She shook her head, turning her black hair alive. 'Everything's wrong.'

'What do you mean?'

'Do you ever think that we were not meant to be together? That the fates were against us from the very beginning, that destiny was against us?'

Her words made no more sense than anything else that had happened today. 'But we have been together—these last nights. We are good together.'

She smiled a smile that told him she agreed, a bittersweet smile that curled her lips and came nowhere near her eyes. 'That's destiny playing tricks again, giving us each other for a few magical hours before twisting the knife in a final, savage act of fate.'

She went to turn away again, but before she could he grabbed her shoulders, wheeling her around. 'What are you talking about? Fate? Destiny? We are together now. You are a widow. I am free to marry whoever I choose. And I choose you, Sera, above all others. I want you to be my wife. I want you to be my queen.'

She pressed her lips together, but he could already see the moisture seeping from her eyes, turning her eyelashes to spikes.

'But I can't marry you, Rafiq.'

Her softly spoken words tore at his heart like razor-sharp claws. 'Can't? Or won't?'

'I can't! And you can't marry me. Not now. Not ever.'

'This makes no sense! Last night you agreed. Last night you said yes. What is the difference now?'

'Because now you will be King!'

He wheeled away. 'This is ridiculous. How do you think I feel about becoming King? Unprepared, raw, inexperienced. Don't you think I could do with someone by my side who has some experience? You were an ambassador's wife for a decade. Don't you think that would help me? God knows I will need help if I am to perform anywhere near what this country needs.'

'No.' Her voice sounded little more than a squeak, with her head bowed low, her chin jammed against her chest. 'I could not help you. Not if you married me.'

The day that had started so badly was getting progressively worse. What could she want? Once upon a time he'd thought her a gold-digger, thought she'd married Hussein for glamour and prestige. He'd accepted that she'd been forced to marry him, and that she'd found a cold marriage bed, but now any lingering thoughts that a rich and opulent lifestyle might somehow still appeal to her died a swift death. Nothing could be more glamorous than the life of a Qusani queen, and yet she was turning that down flat.

'Can you tell me why?'

But she just shook her head. 'I'm sorry. I'm so sorry.'

He wheeled away, his hands tugging at his hair, relishing the sudden pain of it, wishing he could understand what was happening. What the hell did she want? Hadn't he offered her everything last night?

But, no, he hadn't. He hadn't offered her everything because he hadn't realised it then, not until today, when he'd tried to damn Kareef for his actions and found himself justifying them instead. When he'd realised… When he'd *realised*! And it was not too soon to tell her. She felt something for him, he knew. She melted into his touch, became liquid fire in his arms. She must feel something. He just hoped it was not too late to convince her.

He slowly turned back, found her clutching her arms across her belly, tendrils of black hair dancing loose across her wild-eyed face.

'But you have to marry me, Sera, because nobody else will ever do. I love you.'

And her beautiful face crumpled, her keening cry of agony carried away by the wind as she buckled onto her knees in the sand.

'Sera!'

She sobbed without tears into her hand. It was so unfair! He'd spoken of contracts and convenience and sense and sensibilities. He'd made no mention of love when he'd asked her to marry him last night. And she'd agreed, because she wanted him more than anything and it didn't matter if he didn't love her because she would be starting fresh, in a place nobody knew her, and she would have him by her side for ever.

But now to learn he loved her, when she knew she had no choice but to lose him again! There would be no escape, no fresh start, no having Rafiq by her side for ever.

Her lungs squeezed so tight it was near-impossible to breathe. Could this possibly be any harder to bear?

'You can't love me,' she uttered, low and defiant, when the agony in her chest allowed her to continue. 'You mustn't. There's no point.'

'But why?' he asked at her side. 'I know you feel the same. I can feel it.'

And the seeds of escape planted themselves in her mind. Poisoned seeds, perhaps, but not out of character for a woman who was supposed to have poisoned her own husband. Useful in fact, given she had to poison this relationship too. 'That's where you're wrong,' she lied, straightening herself up to stand and dusting off the sand, knowing it would never be so easy to brush memories of this man away. Not after what they'd shared together. 'It was nice to have sex with a real man, I admit—it was definitely a bonus to be relieved of my virginity at last—but I'm frankly surprised a man like you would confuse sex with romance. Because I don't love you, Rafiq. Though I have no doubt there are plenty of women who are already lining up for the opportunity to say they do.'

'You're lying! Tell me you're lying. I command it!'

And somehow, above the shame and hurt and despair, she found the strength to laugh. 'You will make a good king. That much is certain.'

'Tell me!'

'I have told you all I need to hear. I don't love you, Rafiq.'

'Then why did you agree to marry me yesterday?'

She shrugged, her lies tearing her heart apart even as she forced hardness into her features. 'Australia sounded fun. But you'll be stuck here in Qusay now, won't you? I'd be mad to tie myself to you, and you'd be mad to tie yourself to me— given I don't love you, that is.'

Blood crashed in his ears, turned his vision red. It could not be happening again! But he was back there, transported by a thunderbolt through the years, there in that gilded, perfumed hall, a youth with a dream of love for a woman who was his every ideal of perfection.

An ideal that had come crashing down when she had declared to all and sundry that she had never loved him. *Never*.

He was that young man again.

History was repeating itself. His world had once again been split apart. Cruelly. Savagely.

By a woman who didn't deserve his love.

There was a reason you learned from your mistakes, he told himself after he had spun blindly away towards the shell-lined steps to the palace. It was so you wouldn't make the same mistake again. He'd always been proud of his record on that score, always been proud of his ability to learn from his mistakes.

And yet he'd just blown that record, in spectacular style, by begging Sera to marry him—the same woman who had rejected him publicly more than a decade before, the same woman who had just rejected him and his love out of hand once again.

So much for learning from his mistakes.

The sand beneath his feet was too soft, too accommodating to the pounding of his feet. He needed something he could smash, something he could crush under his feet, something he could slam into pieces with his fists.

How could he have been so stupid? How could he have been so blind?

But even as he climbed the stone steps back to the palace, even as the setting sun reflected bright off the shell-rich stone, something sat uneasily with him. For ten years ago she *had* loved him—hadn't he learned as much? And she had said what she had because she'd been forced to marry Hussein and forced to make it look like she actually wanted to.

So why was she saying she couldn't marry him now?

His right foot wavered over a step, the gears crunching in his mind. They were good together—they both knew it—and this time they had more than proved it. And he'd been her first lover, as he'd always intended. Didn't that prove something? That they were meant for each other?

That it was fate that had brought them together again, not fate that was forcing them apart?

Damn it all! Whatever she said, whatever she claimed, this time he wasn't just walking away bitter and twisted and waiting another decade before he found out why. There were enough wasted years between them. There would be no more.

Maybe he had learned from his mistake after all.

He spun around and launched himself down the stairs,

sprinting across the sand to where she sat slumped with her head in her hands.

'Sera!' he cried, and before she could respond he had pulled her to her feet and into his arms. Her eyes were swollen, her cheeks awash with tears and encrusted with grains of sand, but without a doubt she was still the most beautiful woman he'd ever seen. But just one look was enough to make him sure. Enough to let him know he was right.

'Tell me,' he said. 'There is no father this time to intimidate you, no other man you need be afraid of. This time there is only me. So tell me, truthfully this time, why you say you cannot marry me.'

CHAPTER FOURTEEN

SERA collapsed into his arms, her sobs tearing his heart apart, her tears seeping into the cloth of his robe, wetting his skin.

'Oh, Rafiq, I'm so sorry. I...I love you so much!'

They were the words he most needed to hear—so much so that he wanted to roar with victory as he spun her around, his lips on hers a celebration of love shared and hard earned. But he knew there were other words that needed to be said, that he needed to hear, before the way would be clear between them. But it *would* be clear, of that he was sure. He would make damn well sure of it.

'Sera, you must tell me what has been troubling you. I will not leave you another time without knowing. I could not bear it.' His hands stroked her back, soothing, gentling. 'Tell me what's troubling you, and then I can make it right.'

She shook her head. 'There is no righting this. You will want to have nothing to do with me when you know. You will not be able to afford to.'

And he felt a frisson of fear in his gut. *How bad was it?* 'You have to tell me. Everything. Come, sit with me. Explain.' He drew her gently down to the sand, settling her across his lap so he could hold her like a child and kiss her tears away while she spoke.

'Hussein found a use for me,' she began, and Rafiq's blood

ran cold. 'He thought if I was good for nothing else I could help "persuade" visiting delegates to see his point of view. He made me dress like some kind of courtesan, and all the time he was negotiating he would make lewd innuendoes about sex, and how he liked to share what was his.' She stopped, and Rafiq hugged her tight to his chest, wanting to murder the man who had done this to her, who had treated her with such little respect.

'Most of the men were as embarrassed as me. They were family men, they said. They loved their wives. They would leave, barely able to look at me, and Hussein would later say it was because I was not good enough, not pretty enough, that nobody found me attractive enough to sleep with. That I deserved to remain untouched, barren, when I could not even arouse my own husband. And then he would make me try…'

She shuddered, and he sensed her revulsion. 'You don't have to talk about it.'

'You need to know. You need to know it all to understand.' Her voice sounded hollow and empty, as if it was coming from a long, long way away. 'He made me dance, if you could call it that. He watched me from the bed, where he lay naked, and while he— Oh, God, while he tried and tried, and it was my fault that he couldn't—my fault that every time he failed.'

'It's okay,' he soothed, stroking her jet-black hair. 'It's not your fault.'

She blinked up at him, her watery eyes desolate. 'It's not okay. Because by the end I wanted so much for him to succeed I tried to make him come. I thought that maybe then he would be happier. Maybe then he would not be so angry all the other times.'

His hand stilled in her hair, and despite the warmth from the sun a chill descended his spine. 'What other times?'

She buried her head in his chest again, as if too ashamed to look at him. 'There were men who were not such family men, vile men, who believed Hussein was simply being generous, who were only too happy to agree to whatever Hussein wanted for a piece of his wife. But once he had that agreement he would get angry and pretend to take offence, and have them thrown out.'

She jerked in his arms as she gulped in air.

'The ambassador from Karakhistar was one of them. He tried to touch me, brushing his fat fingers through my hair, breathing his ugly hot breath on me, before Hussein had him ejected. He was there today, at the coronation.' She shuddered in his arms. 'I saw him watching me, hating me…'

Rafiq felt sick to the stomach. The enormity of the wrongs against her was inconceivable, and he hugged her closer, trying to replace the hurt, the humiliation. No wonder she'd looked so stricken when he had arrived to take his seat. And no wonder she'd been a shadow of herself when he'd first seen her outside his mother's apartments, unsmiling, her whole body leaden with the abuse Hussein had subjected her to.

Anger simmered in his veins. Because, for all the indignity inflicted upon her, she had remained in the marriage until Hussein had died. 'Why did you do the things you did? Why did you stay with him?'

Again came the quiet, chillingly flat voice. 'I had a kitten he had given me as a wedding present—a perfect Persian kitten, as white as snow. The first time I tried to say no he took it from my hands. He was so angry. I thought he just wanted to get it out of my hands so he could hit me. But he didn't hit me. He didn't need to. One minute he was gently stroking the kitten's fur. The next he had snapped its neck.' She squeezed her eyes shut, her teeth savaging her lip. 'He told me it could just as easily be someone I loved, a friend or one of my family, and I believed him. And then he gave me another kitten the next day.' She looked up at him. 'I tried to save it, Rafiq, I tried to protect it. Believe me, I tried.'

He curled his arms more tightly around her, feeling sick to his stomach. 'What happened?'

'I found it on my pillow, the day Hussein discovered one of the security guards had secretly given me driving lessons. The guard was taken to hospital, bashed senseless. Two lessons! Only two, and that innocent man suffered so much. But Hussein never gave me another kitten after that. He didn't need to.'

Tears flooded her beautiful eyes and he held her close and rocked her, not knowing what else to do, what else to say, until she pushed herself up, swiping tears from her cheeks with the back of her hand. She took a deep breath and then sighed it out.

'And even though Hussein's gone, that's why you can never marry me now. Because as King you will be expected to entertain some of the same people Hussein met, whether it's the ambassador of Karakhistar or any one of a hundred other dignitaries who saw me being offered in exchange for deals and favours. How can they be expected to meet me? For even if they refused, why would they not believe that someone, some time, *would* have taken advantage of Hussein's generous offer? How could such a woman ever be Queen? People will talk. And sooner or later the story will get out. The tabloids would love it. Qusay's Queen, no more than a harlot. The monarchy would become a joke.'

And he pulled her to him, crushing her head to his chest, pressing his lips to her hair, wanting to tell her that she was wrong, wanting to tell her that there was a way out, but finding nothing he could say, nothing he could do.

Because she was right.

The gossip rags would have a field-day.

Damn his brother! For, as much as he had a grudging respect for the strength of character that had seen him choose the woman he loved over a responsibility borne of blood, in doing so his brother had ruined Rafiq's own chance of love.

If Kareef hadn't abdicated they could even now have slipped away to Sydney to live in relative anonymity. But as the Queen Sera would be forced to move in the same social circles as she had with Hussein. It was inevitable that she would run across some of the same men Hussein had offered her to. And, as much as he wanted her as his wife, he had seen her reaction today at the ceremony, and he could not do that to her. And, similarly, he could not expose the monarchy to such scandal.

It would be unworkable. Their marriage would be unworkable. Sera was right. There was no way he could become King, as was his duty, *and* take Sera for his wife.

It didn't stop him trying to work out a way. Lap after lap that evening his swinging arms and kicking legs ate up the pool. Ten laps, then twenty, then thirty, until he had lost count, wanting the pain in his muscles and lungs to overtake the pain in his heart, finally emerging from the pool weak-limbed, with lungs bursting and his mind going over and over the possibilities.

Qusay needed a king to rule over it.

Sera needed a man to love her.

Qusay deserved a king after the hell of the last few weeks.

Sera deserved a lover who could make her forget the hell of her previous marriage.

He fell onto a lounger and dropped his face into a towel. How could he be both lover to Sera and King to Qusay?

And the answer came back in his own fractured heartbeat.

He could not.

But neither was he afforded the ultimate choice Kareef had decided upon: to give up the throne for the woman he loved. With no sign of Tahir, no sightings of his helicopter after days of fruitless searching in the seas around Qusay, he had no option to walk away. He was duty-bound to assume the mantle Kareef had flung in his direction.

This was no mere game of last man standing or pass the parcel. This was about duty and responsibility. The future of a kingdom was at stake and he had no choice.

But why did it have to come at such a cost? Why should he have to give up Sera?

Akmal called for him after a restless night during which he had tossed and turned alone until the early hours, before finally sinking into a fitful sleep. He was being asked for at the hospital, came the message, and, knowing who would be making such an enquiry, Rafiq reluctantly dragged himself from bed and towards the shower.

Sera had refused to sleep with him now that there was no chance they could be together. The sooner they parted, she'd said, the better chance he had to find someone new, someone befitting the title of Sheikha. She would not even accompany him to the hospital. He appreciated her logic even while he doubted it, resenting the thought of having to find another woman when he had her. When he'd *thought* he had her. How exactly was he supposed to sleep with another woman? How could he give that woman children when it was Sera he wanted in his bed, Sera he hungered to see ripe with his child?

'Any news of Tahir?' he asked Akmal as they climbed into the waiting limousine, but Akmal merely shook his head. There was no need for words. Each passing day made the likelihood of his younger brother showing up even slimmer. Rafiq felt the noose tighten ever so slightly around his neck.

Her eyes were closed as he entered her hospital room, but he had the uncanny feeling that even so she missed nothing.

'Prince Rafiq.' It was a surprisingly clear gaze that met his, the curtains gone from her eyes—eyes that shone a startling green, the colour of the very emeralds the women of Marras' worked wonders with. Set amidst her deeply creviced face, they made her look years younger.

'Abizah. It's good to see you again.' He took her gnarled hand. 'Did the operation go well?'

'Thank you so much,' she said, with grateful tears in her eyes, clutching his hand between her own papery-skinned fingers. 'I was hoping you would come, so I could thank you for your generosity. I cannot tell you how wonderful it is for an old woman to see colours and shapes and the beauty of her surroundings.' She looked around, saw only Akmal standing by the door. 'But where is your lovely wife?'

Rafiq drew a sharp breath. Tossed a look at the poker-faced Akmal and wished he'd been in the mountains with them, to hear what Suleman had said about some people thinking she spoke rubbish so that he might understand and not think them both crazy.

'Sera… Sera will visit you later.'

Abizah looked at him with her unclouded eyes, and Rafiq got the impression she could see all the way into his very soul. 'I am sorry. I have caused you sadness by asking when I merely wanted to let you know how much I appreciate your kind gesture.'

'My mother loved your gift,' he said, deflecting the conversation, and at this she smiled.

'Your mother is a fine Sheikha,' she said with a decisive nod, 'as will be our next Queen.'

He turned away. Coming here was pointless. He didn't want to hear about the next queen, no matter how fine she might be, not when it could not be the woman he loved.

'Prince Rafiq, before you go…' He stopped and looked back to the woman on the bed. 'Do not give up hope. Believe. Have faith. There is always an answer.'

Breath whooshed into his lungs as he took a step forward,

his insides flushed with sensation. 'How…? How is it that you see the things you see?'

And she smiled at him, a lifetime of wisdom shining forth from her green eyes. 'Sometimes we look with our eyes and we see only that which is in front of us. Some people have perfect vision but will never see.' She folded her arms and patted her chest. 'For sometimes we must look beyond the pictures our mind presents as fact. Sometimes we need to see what is in our hearts. Only then do we see what is really true.'

He wasn't sure it answered his question. He wasn't sure he understood—but he held onto her words as they made their way back to the palace.

'Sometimes we have to see what is in our hearts.'

Was that what Kareef had done? Listened to his heart and not to his brain? Believed what he felt, rather than what he saw as his duty?

He knew what his brain told him he must do. It was his duty, his responsibility. A king for Qusay.

And yet he knew too what his heart wanted. A black-haired woman with dark eyes and golden skin. The woman who possessed his heart.

Sera.

He had loved and lost her once before. Why should he lose her again?

But who would be king? Who would rule Qusay?

'Believe,' Abizah had said. *'Have faith.'*

He pushed back into the buttery leather upholstery and took a deep breath. The old woman was right. By the time the car pulled up outside the glistening palace he knew what he had to do.

'Akmal,' he said, stopping the vizier from alighting with a hand to his arm. 'There's been a change of plans.'

CHAPTER FIFTEEN

HE RAN through the palace, along the long cloistered walkways fragrant with citrus and frangipani and a thousand exotic flowers whose heady scent perfumed the air. He ran up the steps to the wing that housed his mother's apartment, scattering cooing pigeons in a flurry of feathers and flapping wings.

'Sera!' he called, banging on the door. 'Sera. I need to talk to you.'

And then the door opened and she was there, her eyes confused, still puffy. 'What's happened, Rafiq? What's wrong?'

He spun her in his arms. 'Nothing is wrong. Everything is wonderfully, perfectly right.'

She laughed uncertainly. 'What are you talking about? Have they found Tahir?' For a moment he faltered, but only for a moment. 'They will,' he said, believing it in his heart, 'but this isn't about him. This is about you and me. We're getting married.'

'But, Rafiq, we can't. You know we can't. There is no way—'

'There *is* a way, Sera. There is one way, and I am taking it.'

Shock transformed her face. 'You can't renounce the crown! Not after Kareef. You would be denying your very birthright.'

'Is it my birthright? I have never once in my life thought bout taking over the reins of Qusay. It was a thought as foreign to me as this very land became when I adopted another as my home. And now, to find that circumstances have thrust me into this position—how is that a birthright?'

'But, Rafiq, you would be throwing away your future.'

'No, Sera, I would be reclaiming it. For *you* are my future and always have been. Because from the moment we met we were meant to be together—as surely as the sand belongs to the desert and the mountain peaks to the sky. We are part of each other and always will be.'

'Rafiq, think of what you are doing…'

'I know exactly what I am doing. I lost you once before and I will not lose you again.' He went down on one knee before her. 'I love you, Sera. Marry me. Be my wife. Live my future alongside me.'

Tears welled in her beautiful dark eyes, but there was love there too, love that swelled his heart and gave him hope. For if she denied him he would be a broken man. A king with no queen. Adrift and alone.

'Oh, Rafiq, I love you so much. You have given my life colour again when I thought there would be none. You have given me back my heart.'

'Then you'll marry me?'

And she nodded, her lips tightly pressed. 'Yes, Rafiq—oh, yes, I'll marry you!'

He was still kissing her when his mother bustled in, calling for Sera. She stopped, wide-eyed, when she found them, the excitement in her eyes masked by questions for no more than a second. 'You're both here, how wonderful. Have you heard the news? A helicopter's been found in the desert. Akmal's gone straight there. They think it might be Tahir's!' She wrung her hands nervously in front of her. 'And to think that all this time we thought he just hadn't bothered to come. Do you think…? Is there any chance…?'

And Rafiq wondered if this day could get any better as he put an arm around her shoulders and brought her into his embrace—the two women he loved most in the world held within the circle of his arms. 'Believe,' he told her, remembering the words of the wise woman, the woman their firstborn daughter would be named for. 'Have faith.'

EPILOGUE

SYDNEY society had seen nothing like it. The dress was made of a spun gold fabric laden with emerald chips, the best the craftswomen of Marrash had to offer, and the design an ancient Qusani pattern that meant, so Rafiq had been assured, prosperity, long life, and—most important apparently—fertility. Fitted to the waist, it fell in skilfully constructed folds to the ground. The gown was both elegant and timeless, a blend of the best of the east and the west, and with a veil of gold over her black hair she looked like a gift from the gods.

His gift from the gods.

Rafiq tried to contain his joy as she neared. Others could not. The group of tribespeople flown in especially from Marrash to one side, Abizah among them, called blessings as she passed, remarking on her beauty, sending their good wishes in voices that sounded in this place of worship like song.

Other guests, thinking this some quaint Qusani custom, joined in, so that Sera joined his side not to the sound of organ music but to the sound of a thousand blessings ringing out through the chapel.

It was a wedding the likes of which Sydney had never seen before, he thought, and nor was it likely to see again. It was a wedding where the guests responded spontaneously and the whole world rejoiced as it was transmitted around the globe. The guest list had been carefully handpicked, so there could be no embarrassment, no humiliation on either side.

It was the wedding, as far as he was concerned, to end all weddings.

Rafiq smiled down at her as she drew near, curled her hand in his, and she beamed up at him with what looked like her whole heart.

'I love you,' he said, knowing those words were more true in this very moment than ever before.

His black-haired beauty looked up at him, nothing but love shining out at him from her dark eyes. 'As I love you, Rafiq. Forever.'

And his heart swelled. Who needed to be king, he wondered, when you already had your queen?

HARLEQUIN *Presents*

Coming Next Month

Coming Next Month

LARGER-PRINT BOOKS!

HARLEQUIN *Presents*

PASSION GUARANTEED SEDUCTION

GET 2 FREE LARGER-PRINT NOVELS PLUS 2 FREE GIFTS!

YES! Please send me 2 FREE LARGER-PRINT Harlequin Presents® novels and my 2 FREE gifts (gifts are worth about $10). After receiving them, if I don't wish to receive any more books, I can return the shipping statement marked "cancel." If I don't cancel, I will receive 6 brand-new novels every month and be billed just $4.55 per book in the U.S. or $5.24 per book in Canada. That's a saving of at least 13% off the cover price! It's quite a bargain! Shipping and handling is just 50¢ per book.* I understand that accepting the 2 free books and gifts places me under no obligation to buy anything. I can always return a shipment and cancel at any time. Even if I never buy another book, the two free books and gifts are mine to keep forever.

176/376 HDN E5NG

Name	(PLEASE PRINT)	
Address		Apt. #
City	State/Prov	Zip/Postal Code

Signature (if under 18, a parent or guardian must sign)

Mail to the Harlequin Reader Service:
IN U.S.A.: P.O. Box 1867, Buffalo, NY 14240-1867
IN CANADA: P.O. Box 609, Fort Erie, Ontario L2A 5X3

Not valid for current subscribers to Harlequin Presents Larger-Print books.

**Are you a subscriber to Harlequin Presents books and want to receive the larger-print edition?
Call 1-800-873-8635 today!**

* Terms and prices subject to change without notice. Prices do not include applicable taxes. Sales tax applicable in N.Y. Canadian residents will be charged applicable provincial taxes and GST. Offer not valid in Quebec. This offer is limited to one order per household. All orders subject to approval. Credit or debit balances in a customer's account(s) may be offset by any other outstanding balance owed by or to the customer. Please allow 4 to 6 weeks for delivery. Offer available while quantities last.

Your Privacy: Harlequin Books is committed to protecting your privacy. Our Privacy Policy is available online at www.eHarlequin.com or upon request from the Reader Service. From time to time we make our lists of customers available to reputable third parties who may have a product or service of interest to you. If you would prefer we not share your name and address, please check here. ☐

Help us get it right—We strive for accurate, respectful and relevant communications. To clarify or modify your communication preferences, visit us at www.ReaderService.com/consumerschoice.

HPLP10R

HARLEQUIN®

A Romance

FOR EVERY MOOD™

Spotlight on

Heart & Home

Heartwarming romances
where love can happen
right when you least expect it.

See the next page to enjoy a sneak peek
from Silhouette Special Edition®,
a Heart and Home series.

Introducing McFARLANE'S PERFECT BRIDE
by USA TODAY *bestselling author Christine Rimmer,*
from Silhouette Special Edition®.

Entranced. Captivated. Enchanted.

Connor sat across the table from Tori Jones and couldn't help thinking that those words exactly described what effect the small-town schoolteacher had on him. He might as well stop trying to tell himself he wasn't interested. He was powerfully drawn to her.

Clearly, he should have dated more when he was younger.

There had been a couple of other women since Jennifer had walked out on him. But he had never been entranced. Or captivated. Or enchanted.

Until now.

He wanted her—*her,* Tori Jones, in particular. Not just someone suitably attractive and well-bred, as Jennifer had been. Not just someone sophisticated, sexually exciting and discreet, which pretty much described the two women he'd dated after his marriage crashed and burned.

It came to him that he…he *liked* this woman. And that was new to him. He liked her quick wit, her wisdom and her big heart. He liked the passion in her voice when she talked about things she believed in.

He liked *her.* And suddenly it mattered all out of proportion that she might like him, too.

Was he losing it? He couldn't help but wonder. Was he cracking under the strain—of the soured economy, the McFarlane House setbacks, his divorce, the scary changes in his son? Of the changes he'd decided he needed to make in his life and himself?

Strangely, right then, on his first date with Tori Jones, he didn't care if he just might be going over the edge. He was having a great time—having *fun*, of all things—and he didn't want it to end.

Is Connor finally able to admit his feelings to Tori, and are they reciprocated?
Find out in McFARLANE'S PERFECT BRIDE
by USA TODAY bestselling author Christine Rimmer.
Available July 2010,
only from Silhouette Special Edition®.

SSEEXP0710

HARLEQUIN®
Super Romance®

Top author
Janice Kay Johnson

brings readers a heartwarming
small-town story

with

CHARLOTTE'S
HOMECOMING

After their father is badly injured on the farm,
Faith Russell calls her estranged twin sister,
Charlotte, to return to the small rural town she
escaped so many years ago. When Charlotte
falls for Gray Van Dusen, the handsome town
mayor, her feelings of home begin to change.
As the relationship grows, will Charlotte
finally realize that there is no better place
than *home?*

Available in July
wherever books are sold.

HARLEQUIN®

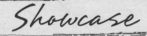
Showcase

LESLIE KELLY
Naturally Naughty

Wicked & Willing

On sale June 8

Reader favorites from the most talented voices in romance

Save $1.00 on the purchase of 1 or more Harlequin® Showcase books.

SAVE $1.00 on the purchase of 1 or more Harlequin® Showcase books.

Coupon expires November 30, 2010. Redeemable at participating retail outlets.
Limit one coupon per customer. Valid in the U.S.A. and Canada only.

52609057

5 65373 00076 2   (8100)0 11654

HSCCOUP0610